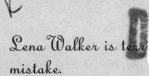

Lena Walker is terr... *mistake.*

Fear gripped her like the time she'd sighted a cloud of grasshoppers descending on the fields ready for harvest. Gabriel Hunters was nothing like she'd pictured: He didn't look like he'd ever spent a day in his life on a farm. Well, she simply had to know the truth.

"Did you grow up on a farm?" she asked.

"Not exactly," he replied after a moment's pause.

The fright subsided to a rising anger. "Where then did you learn about it?"

"From books," he said simply, staring straight ahead.

His reply shook the very foundation on which she built her values. "From books? How can you feel the soil between your fingertips from a book? How can you tell the color of ripe wheat?"

"The written word is a valuable asset. I place complete trust in what I've read and studied." His ample chest rose and fell, while the buttons on his jacket threatened to break free. "Man has farmed since the beginning of time. If it were a difficult process, then human beings would not have survived."

I refuse to lose my temper. She clucked the horses to venture a tad faster. *I refuse to lose my temper.* "Many people have died due to crop failures or the natural hardships arising from living here. I hope you read *that* in your books."

"I have."

"And your conclusion, good sir?" She gritted her teeth to keep from adding a vicious retort.

"I have determined to be a farmer. There are many things for me to put into practice from the books I've read. If I had thought this undertaking an impossibility, I would not have answered your advertisement."

Mercy. What have I done?

DIANN MILLS draws the broken to wholeness in her writing. She lives in Houston, Texas, with her husband, Dean. She wrote from the time she could hold a pencil, but not seriously until God made it clear that she should write for Him. After three years of serious writing, her first book, *Rehoboth,* won favorite **Heartsong Presents** historical for 1998. Other publishing credits include magazine articles and short stories, devotionals, poetry, and internal writing for her church. She is a founding board member of American Christian Romance Writers, speaks for various groups, and conducts writing workshops. She is an active church choir member, leads a ladies' Bible study, and is a church librarian.

Books by DiAnn Mills

HEARTSONG PRESENTS

Don't miss out on any of our super romances. Write to us at the following address for information on our newest releases and club membership.

Heartsong Presents Readers' Service
PO Box 721
Uhrichsville, OH 44683

Or visit www.heartsongpresents.com

Mail-Order Husband

DiAnn Mills

Heartsong Presents

To Lane and Katie Dyke and their precious children,
Hannah, Hayley, Jim Bob, and Jenni Beth.
Many thanks to Meredith Efken
for her valuable assistance in researching Nebraska.

A note from the author:
*I love to hear from my readers! You may correspond with me
by writing:*

DiAnn Mills
Author Relations
PO Box 719
Uhrichsville, OH 44683

ISBN 1-58660-618-2

MAIL-ORDER HUSBAND

All Scripture quotations are taken from the King James Version of
the Bible.

All of the characters and events in this book are fictitious. Any
resemblance to actual persons, living or dead, or to actual events
is purely coincidental.

Cover illustration © GettyOne.

PRINTED IN THE U.S.A.

prologue

Central Nebraska, 1880

Lena Walker stiffened and glared into the face of the man before her. "I will not marry you, Dagget Shafer. Not now, not tomorrow, not ever."

His small, dark eyes narrowed, and despite the thick black beard covering most of his face, skin as bright red as a cardinal's feathers shone through. "You will change your mind, Miz High and Mighty. You can't run this farm by yourself and rear those two younguns. You'll either starve or get sick and die."

"I can work this land and raise my children just fine by myself," she said with a lift of her chin. Perspiration beaded her forehead and trickled down her back as she fought her rising temper.

"I dare say you'll live to regret your decision not to marry me. A woman needs a man to take care of her and tell her what to do," he shot back. "And if you had the sense to look around, you'd see there ain't many eligible men in these parts." He turned to face the entrance of the sod dugout, used as a barn, then whirled back around. "Of course, now I see you'd make a bad wife. I need a woman who knows the meanin' of doin' what her husband says and where her place is, not some sassy, purdy face. Miz Walker, you ain't got what I need. You ain't fit for any man."

Swallowing another sharp retort, Lena glanced at the bucket of water in her hands and, without thinking, tossed the contents into Dagget Shafer's face. Probably the closest

5

thing he'd seen to a bath in a year. "Get off my land." Venom riddled her voice. "We don't need the likes of you."

For a minute she thought Dagget might strike her. She dropped the bucket, grabbed the pitchfork leaning against the dugout wall, and silently dared him to step closer.

Dagget must have sensed she meant business because he plodded toward his mule, muttering something she couldn't make out.

Lena started to challenge his view of her fitness to be a wife but held her tongue. She'd run him off, and that's what she'd intended. How could he think she'd be interested in a man who never bathed, had the manners of a pig, and refused to step inside a church? Her heart ached for his six children who no longer had a mother, but her sympathy didn't extend to marrying their unbearable father.

"Mama, you all right?" eleven-year-old Caleb asked, peering around the corner of a horse stall.

She took a deep breath to settle her pounding heart as Dagget rode away, his legs flapping against the sides of the mule. "Yes, Son. I'll be fine."

He picked up the empty bucket. "I'll go fetch some more water."

Lena nodded and laid her hand on her son's shoulder. "Thanks, Caleb."

He glanced up through serious, sky-blue eyes. "I'm glad you're not marryin' him, Mama. We do just fine by ourselves."

Suddenly the whole incident seemed funny. The thought of Dagget standing there with water dripping from his greasy beard to his dirty overalls, nary saying a word, was priceless. Caleb took to laughing too, and their mirth echoed from the sod barn's walls.

"We do need help," Lena finally admitted. "But it will be by God's hand, not by Dagget Shafer or any of the others who seem to think I'm begging for a husband."

"We work good together, Mama," Caleb insisted.

She smiled into the face of the boy who looked so much like his departed father, with the same dark brown hair and tall, lanky frame. "Right now, you, Simon, and I are doing all right, but tomorrow may bring something else. God will provide; I'm sure of it. But I need to talk to Him about the matter."

That night, after the embers from the cow chips no longer produced a flicker of orange-red, and the only sounds around her were her sons' even breathing, Lena prayed for guidance.

Oh, Lord, what do You want me to do? This place needs a man to run it, and the boys are too young. I know the men who have come asking me to marry them could run this farm proper, but Lord, none of them were fit. She shook her head in the darkness, dispelling the visions of the other two farmers who had indicated a desire to marry her. One of them was old enough to be her father, and the other reminded her of a billy goat—with a disposition to match.

Lord, Dagget made me awful angry today, and I'm sorry to have lost my temper. I'll apologize the next time I see him; I promise. It's my pride, I know. I'm sorry, and I'll do better.

Life simply didn't seem fair. Men could come looking for a wife, even place a notice in one of those big newspapers back East. They took advantage of women who had no one to help them when circumstances took a bad turn.

Suddenly an idea occurred to her. If a man could find himself a bride by placing an advertisement, why couldn't she find a husband?

one

Wanted: Christian husband for widow with two young boys. Must be of high moral character, refrain from drinking spirits, be even-tempered, and be able to run a farm in central Nebraska. Interested gentlemen apply by mail. Please allow two to three months for reply.

Gabriel Hunters smoothed out the wrinkled *Philadelphia Public Ledger* advertisement. He'd read it several times during the past three days and had committed the words to memory. Tonight he'd crumpled it, certain the foolish notion would pass once the paper crackled in the fireplace.

But Gabriel couldn't rid himself of the hope bubbling between the lines of the print. He snatched the newspaper clipping from the sputtering flames, as though the words were more valuable than silver or gold.

Something foreign had occurred to him, something contrary to his hermetic way of life. He actually wanted to respond positively to this widow. A big part of him believed a home and family might fill the emptiness in his heart. Shaking his head, Gabriel suspected God had plans for his perfunctory existence, and the thought brought a surge of unusual emotions. He felt a strange and exhilarating strength in considering a home beyond Philadelphia. Many times he'd wondered what lay outside his world of private bookkeeping, a place where gossip and malicious speech didn't prevail.

Glancing about the sparsely furnished room, he concluded nothing really held him in Philadelphia. Mother had passed away two years prior, and his best friends—his books—could be taken with him. God could be providing a way to obliterate the past and start anew. Certainly a pleasurable thought.

Allowing himself to dream a trifle, Gabriel closed his eyes and imagined the tantalizing aroma of beef stew and baking bread, the sound of children's laughter, and the sweet smile of a woman who loved him.

He studied the newspaper clipping again. What did he know about being a husband and rearing children? He'd never courted a woman or known his own father. After much thought, he realized men had been husbands and fathers for thousands of years. Certainly it came natural.

Another thought occurred to him. Jesus was not much younger than Gabriel when He embarked upon His ministry. Perhaps this stood as a sign from God to answer affirmatively to the widow's notice. He could do this; the Bible would be his guide.

The dilemma lay in farming. He rubbed his hands together. Soft. No calluses. Mother had insisted upon a small garden behind her establishment, but all he'd done was pick a few tomatoes and green beans. The girls had managed the rest. All the work he'd ever accomplished amounted to dipping his quill into an inkwell. Gabriel grinned. *The Farmers Almanac* provided all the knowledge he might ever need to till the land. How difficult could it be to milk a cow or plant seeds and harvest crops? After all, men had tilled the earth since Adam and Eve. He'd spent most of his life submerged in books and had learned volumes of vital information, and he felt confident in his savvy. This new venture merely challenged his intellectual appetite.

Gabriel stood and stepped away from his oaken desk. He surmised Lena Walker must not be endowed with qualities of beauty or she wouldn't have had to resort to advertising for a husband. It didn't matter, for he certainly had not been given eye-pleasing traits either.

A husband and father. Something he'd secretly dreamed of becoming but had never thought he'd share in the blessing.

ዼ

Monday, October 14, 1880

Lena pulled her frayed, woolen shawl around her shoulders as a north wind whipped around the train station. She shivered, not relishing an early winter, but at least she'd have a husband to keep the fires burning and a helpmate to share in the work. How pleasant to think of conversation with someone other than two young sons—not that she didn't appreciate their willingness to talk—but sometimes she felt hauntingly alone.

"Mama, I hear it," Caleb said, glancing up from where he'd bent his ear to the train track.

"I do too," six-year-old Simon chimed in.

Lena felt her heart pound harder than the rhythmic sound of the Union Pacific making its way toward Archerville, a small town north of Lincoln and not far from the Platte River. Fear gripped her. What had she done? Ever since she'd accepted Gabriel Hunters's aspirations to marry her and be a father to her sons, she'd begun to have serious doubts. Up until she'd posted her reply, the idea had sounded like a fantasy, a perfect solution to all of her woes. Of course she'd prayed for direction and felt God had led her to Mr. Hunters, but could she have misunderstood God?

Her stomach twisted and turned. This man could be a vagrant or, worse yet, an outlaw intending on doing harm to her and her precious sons. Advertising for a husband now sounded foolish. Accepting a man's proposal sight unseen sounded even worse. She'd be the laughingstock of the community, and that didn't help her prideful nature.

What had happened to her faith? Hadn't she heard clear direction from God about the matter? She'd received more than twenty replies from interested men, but none had piqued her interest like the man she expected on board the train. With a name like Gabriel Hunters, he must be the strong, burly type. In fact, his name lent itself to that of a lumberjack. Yes, a rugged wilderness man who lived by his cunning and wits.

Swallowing hard, she forced a smile in the direction of her lively sons. *Oh, Lord, make Mr. Hunters a likeable man who'll love my boys. They can be a handful, but oh, what joy.* Both looked identical to their father, but Caleb leaned more to a compassionate nature, and Simon always ran with the wind and whatever notion that entered his mind.

"It's getting closer," Simon said nearly squealing. "I wonder what Mr. Hunters looks like."

"I'm wondering if he'll be friendly," Caleb said in a chiding tone. "That's more important."

"He'll be whatever the good Lord desires for us," Lena said. "And the Lord only wants the best for His children."

She felt her mouth grow dry as the train chugged down the tracks, slowly coming to a halt and carrying the inevitable. Naturally if the man proved to be less than she expected, she'd refuse to wed him. They weren't to be married until three days hence, which gave both of them time to consider what the future held in store. She wanted to pray with him and talk about everything. No surprises for Lena. Mr. Hunters might be taking on a ready-made family, but he was also getting a farm.

Remembering his letter tucked inside her pocket, she fingered it lightly. His penned words echoed across her mind.

Dear Mrs. Walker,

This correspondence is in regards to your advertisement for a husband and father for your sons. I am thirty-six years old and have never been married, but I believe God will show me through His Word how to be a proper husband and father. I abstain from strong drink or tobacco, and I welcome the opportunity to share in your family's life and teach your sons what little I know.

I've studied agricultural methods and am prepared to be of assistance in this endeavor. I'm a modest man and

*not easily persuaded, but God has put our union in my
heart.*

Sincerely,
Gabriel Hunters

Lena assumed Mr. Hunters had an excellent education
from his choice of words. How magnificent for her sons. She
felt truly blessed and exhilarated—until the train's whistle
sounded, the steam billowed with a *spwish,* and the train
screeched to a halt.

Lena well knew her ability to act hastily. *Oh, Lord. I'm
afraid I've made a terrible mistake. Please give me a sign.*

A man stepped down from the train, a tall, stout fellow who
hadn't been able to fasten his jacket. A gust of wind caused
him to suck in his breath. Wiry, yellow hair, resembling straw,
stuck out haphazardly from beneath a tattered hat as though he
might take flight. A patch of the same barbed-wire hair sprang
up from his eyebrows, ample jaws, and chin.

Lena covered her mouth to keep from laughing, but then
she saw no other man exiting the train. Oh, my, what *had*
she done?

The man set his bag beside him and removed his hat,
clutching it close to his heart. His hair lay matted like wet
chicken feathers. "Mrs. Walker," he said, approaching her
with a concerned frown. "Are you Mrs. Lena Walker?"

"Yes, I am," she replied and extended her hand. He grasped
it lightly. It felt cold and clammy. Lena dare not look at Caleb
and Simon for fear she'd burst into laughter—or tears.

"I'm Gabriel Hunters," he said with a gulp, his words
jumping out like a squeak.

"It's a pleasure to meet you, Mr. Hunters." She released
her hand and gestured toward her sons. "This is Caleb; he's
eleven. And this is Simon; he's six."

*Oh, Lord, help them to remember their manners. Help me
to remember mine!*

Mr. Hunters bent his portly frame and offered his hand first to Caleb, then to Simon. "It's an honor to meet you, Caleb and Simon Walker. I'm looking forward to an auspicious relationship."

His voice trembled slightly, and Lena felt compassion tug at her heart. She hadn't considered he might have reservations about their meeting.

Simon's gaze shot up at his mother. "Are we in trouble, Mama?"

Lena gathered her shawl closer to her; the wind had taken a colder twist. "I don't think so, Son." She took a deep breath, hoping her ignorance didn't show through. "Mr. Hunters, Simon isn't sure of the meaning of auspicious."

Still bending at the knee, he nodded and turned his attention to the small boy. "It means successful or promising."

Simon's blue eyes appeared to radiate with understanding. "Mama says a word like that when she thinks Caleb and I are doing something we shouldn't."

"Suspicious?" Mr. Hunters asked.

"Yes, Sir. That's it. Do you like chores, Mr. Hunters? Me and Caleb get real tired of 'em, and we're sure glad you're here to help." He reached out to shake Mr. Hunters's hand again. "I see you like to eat a lot, Sir, and your clothes appear a bit tight, but never you mind. Our mama cooks real good, and she can fix your clothes when they tear."

"Simon," Lena gasped, horrified. Hadn't they talked about proper introductions all the way to Archerville?

Mr. Hunters stood and tugged at his gaping jacket. "I apologize if my corpulent body is offensive."

"No, Sir. Not in the least," Lena replied before one of the boys could embarrass her further. She assumed the meaning of corpulent had something to do with his size. "Kindly excuse my son's bad manners. Caleb, would you like to carry Mr. Hunters's bag to the wagon? We can all get to know each other on the way home, and I'll cook supper while you boys show

Mr. Hunters around the farm."

Mr. Hunters stared anxiously at the train. "I have another bag, but it's extremely cumbersome. Several of my books are packed inside."

As if hearing the man's words, the conductor scooted out a fairly large trunk. "Right heavy this is," he said, massaging the small of his back.

Mr. Hunters reached for his belongings and stumbled with the weight. Lena dashed forward with Caleb and Simon, but the man fell flat on his back with his bag quivering atop his chest and rounded stomach.

Instantly, the conductor stood by his side and removed the trunk, then helped the dazed man to his feet. Simon began to chuckle, followed by Caleb. Despite Lena's stern looks, the two boys laughed even harder. She found it difficult to contain herself, wanting to give in to the mirth tickling through her body. *Oh, Lord, surely I misunderstood!*

"Oh dear, are you all right?" she asked, trying desperately to gain control of her wavering emotions.

Mr. Hunters shrugged his shoulders and dusted off his clothes. "Ma'am, this is definitely not the proper image I wanted to present you. I sincerely apologize for my blunder."

"No need to fret about it," she said, and for the first time she caught a glimpse of his eyes—coppery brown, much like the color of autumn leaves, unusual for a person with blond hair. A second look reminded her of a frightened animal, cornered with no place to run.

Poor Mr. Hunters, and we're laughing at him. Immediately, she sobered. "I hope you don't mind, but I scheduled the wedding for three days hence. I thought we could use the time to get accustomed to each other."

His face turned ghastly white. "Ma'am—"

Lena gathered what had shocked him. "Sir, I intended to have you sleep in the barn until our wedding." Her face grew hotter than a Nebraska sun in mid-July.

He released a pent-up breath. "Those arrangements sound perfectly fine to me."

They moved awkwardly toward Lena's wagon. Caleb and Simon struggled with one bag, and Mr. Hunters heaved with the trunk. Moments before, Simon had embarrassed her with his endless prattle. Now no one uttered a word.

"You must be quite fond of books," she said, groping for something to say.

"Yes, Ma'am. I hope you don't mind, but I took the liberty of having the rest of them sent here in a few weeks."

"Of course not. The winter nights approaching us will provide you with plenty of reading time."

"Will you read these books to us, Sir?" Caleb asked, struggling with the heavy bag.

Mr. Hunters's shoulders relaxed. "I'd be pleased to, along with the Bible."

Lena swallowed. Mr. Hunters might not be what she envisioned, but this part of him was a relief.

They reached the wagon and, after much difficulty, loaded the trunk and bag. Caleb and Simon climbed into the back, curiously eyeing the outside of Mr. Hunters's baggage.

"Do not touch those," she reminded them.

Lena turned for the man to assist her onto the wagon seat, which he did with much effort. Huffing and puffing, he attempted a smile.

"Would you like to drive us west toward my home?" she asked, smoothing her dress.

His shoulders sank. "Ma'am, I've never driven a wagon before in my life."

two

Gabriel wanted to step down from that wagon and make a running leap to board the Union Pacific back to Philadelphia as fast as his round and aching legs would allow.

His entrance into Archerville had been met with one disaster after another—and this last occurrence would surely conclude his demise. The boys, his future sons, had been beset with amusement when the trunk landed him on his backside, and his future wife had just learned he knew nothing about driving a wagon.

Defeated and exhausted from the laborious trip to middle-of-nowhere Nebraska, Gabriel realized he'd made a terrible mistake. And in three days' time, he might make an even worse one.

Oh, God, why did I think You willed this for my life? Am I once again to be made a laughingstock of a community?

"Don't concern yourself, Mr. Hunters. I've driven this wagon more times than I care to remember," Mrs. Walker said, but he couldn't tell if she sounded annoyed or simply tired—most likely the former.

He didn't blame her; he wasn't pleased with his lack of dexterity either. In less than ten minutes, he'd discovered that not all knowledge came from books. Apprehension rippled through him at the likelihood of the next twenty-four hours revealing a generous amount of his ignorance.

"Mr. Hunters," Caleb began. "What did you do while in Philadelphia?"

Obviously he didn't drive a team of horses.

"Bookkeeping," Gabriel replied. When he saw the rather confused look spreading across the boy's face, he added,

16

"It's arithmetic. I help business establishments add and subtract what they earn and what they spend."

Caleb nodded. "Like when Mama sells a cow, then pays our bill at the general store?"

"Correct, and what's left is profit."

"We don't have any of that," Caleb said with a much-too-serious look for a boy. "We simply pay what's owed and start all over again."

Gabriel saw a muscle twitch in Mrs. Walker's face. Farming a 160-acre homestead and raising two boys must be a real hardship. No wonder she needed a husband. At least she knew how to survive. His former confidence in farming had ended at the railroad station.

"But the Lord provides," Lena said quietly. "We have a house, clothes to wear, and food. Some folks aren't as fortunate."

"I pray I'll be able to make you more prosperous," Gabriel said firmly.

"Thank you, Mr. Hunters. I—"

"Are we going to be rich?" Simon asked, tugging on Gabriel's coattail. "I know zactly what I want."

"Simon," Mrs. Walker scolded. "Mind your manners. Now, you boys leave Mr. Hunters alone for awhile. He and I have things to discuss."

The boys scooted back to the end of the wagon and dangled their feet over the edge. They minded well. A good sign. He'd seen his share of misbehaved boys and the damage they could do.

Gabriel glanced at the sights of Archerville behind him as they pulled away from the small town. One dusty street was lined with a few necessary businesses: a general store and post office; a jail; a barber and undertaker; a saloon; and across from the liquid spirits and worldly entertainment, a freshly painted church—for a dose of the Holy Ghost.

The odor staggered him. Horses, pigs, and cows wandered through the town and contributed their droppings wherever they saw fit. Certainly nothing resembling the cleanliness or the hustle and bustle of Philadelphia. A burst of wind whipped around a barrel outside the general store, sending it teetering to the ground. A shiver wound its way around Gabriel's spine. As much as he'd looked forward to leaving the city, this new environment settled upon him like questionable figures in a ledger.

He'd been lonely before with people everywhere, but now he felt alone and afraid. Yes, fear did have a strangling hold on him, fear of the unknown and fear of the future. God did lead him here to Archerville, of that he had no doubt, but those thoughts did little to calm him.

Gabriel studied Mrs. Walker's horses. They appeared fine to him—shiny coats and not at all swaybacked. He'd expected mules. His gaze trailed up the reins to her hands, callused and deeply tanned. He'd never seen a woman's hands that weren't soft and smooth. Another oddity. Well, he didn't intend for his wife to work herself into an early grave. Wetting his lips, he stole a quick glance at her face. With all the commotion at the train station, he hadn't afforded a good look at his future wife.

Oh no. Shocked and disgruntled, he instantly changed his focus to the surrounding countryside, flat, bleak, and uninviting.

Lena Walker was comely, and he couldn't trust an attractive woman. She'd betray him just like his mother and the other girls. For weeks since he'd received Mrs. Walker's agreement to the marriage, he'd prayed for a plain woman, one who matched him in appearance. A man could build a life with a woman who'd never stray. He'd never have to worry about her participating in the activities his mother had.

Suddenly, Gabriel fought the urge to shake his fist at God. The One in whom he'd put his faith and trust had tricked him. He'd journeyed all this way only to find a woman who would hurt him more deeply than his mother. Although his mother had died and he'd forgiven her, he was smart enough not to fall into the same well again.

What should he do now? *Lord, cruel jokes are what the bullies did when I attended school. I can't believe this is from You. Even if she might be different, she'd never love the likes of me. Have You forgotten what I look like?*

"Mr. Hunters, forgive me. I had so many things to ask you, but now I can't seem to figure out where to begin." Mrs. Walker offered him a slight smile, then quickly stared ahead at the road.

Perhaps you're disappointed; can't blame you. "We're strangers, Mrs. Walker. We have much to learn about each other."

"Yes, that's true. Could we begin by calling each other by our given names and talking about ourselves?"

He nodded, although not so sure he wanted Lena Walker to know more about him. "Certainly, if it suits you."

She took a deep breath and sat straighter as though summoning courage for an arduous task. "My name is Lena Jane Walker. My family came to Nebraska from Ohio when I was a girl. I'll be thirty-one years old come February." She paused and urged the team of horses to pick up their pace. "I've been a widow for three years. I'm strong and healthy, and so are my sons. The Lord guides my life, but I do tend to make mistakes more often than not."

"We all do," he said solemnly, regretting the moment he'd considered her advertisement for a husband. Why hadn't she told him what she looked like?

"My biggest fault is my temper," she continued, as though bound by some unexplainable force to confess her worst. "I'll do my best to curb it, but I thought you should know."

When she looked his way again, the intensity of her green eyes captured his heart. Their gazes locked, and he could not pull away. Truth and sincerity with a mixture of merriment radiated back at him. The combination caused Gabriel to rethink his former conclusions about comely women. *Help, I'm so confused.*

Could it be Lena Walker held no malice? He knew God intended the best for him, and for a moment, Gabriel had forgotten His goodness. He'd proceed with caution, remembering more than one of his mother's girls had looked innocent as a child.

Mrs. Walker averted his scrutiny. "I want you to know the real reason why I contacted the Philadelphia newspaper."

"I'd be obliged if you would. Naturally, I assumed you needed help with your land and your sons."

"Yes, but I never thought a man would be interested in coming all this way, and when you did, I took it as a sign from God that this was His will. You see, two farmers asked me to marry, but I couldn't tolerate them. I felt advertising for a husband made more sense. I wanted God to send what I needed."

His stomach lunged. "Why didn't you wed one of the men who proposed?"

She shrugged. "They weren't God-fearing, or bathed, or good to my sons. When they came around asking, I threw them off my land. Guess they got a taste of my temper."

A mental picture of this woman tossing a grown man off her farm leaped from his mind. It sounded incredibly funny, and he stifled a laugh.

"You can laugh," she said, shaking her head. "Most folks around here do anyway. They think I've lost my mind by refusing to marry up with a man who'd take care of the farm." She stopped talking abruptly, as though she suddenly felt embarrassed.

Gabriel thought about Lena's confession, and a cloud darkened his mind. "Ma'am, are you desiring a husband who allows you to direct his ways?" *I may not be handsome or successful, but I believe a man is head of his household.*

Lena abruptly reined the horses to a halt. Her face paled. "By no means. I believe in the biblical instructions for husbands and wives—a husband guides and directs his home."

"As I do. A marriage must follow every God-given precept."

"Precisely. Now, tell me about yourself."

The tension seemed to grow worse. He didn't want or see a reason to reveal much about his person. He deemed a willingness to do right by her was all that held importance. "You already know quite a bit about me from our correspondence. My complete name is Gabriel Lawrence Hunters, and I've lived my whole life in Philadelphia."

"Are your parents living?"

"Mother passed on some two years ago."

"So your father is still in Philadelphia?"

Gracious, Woman, how much do you need to know about me? "I have no idea." He prayed for a diversion, anything to stop the questioning. "This is magnificent country."

She smiled. "Yes, it is. In late summer, prairie grass can grow taller than a man."

He studied the landscape in curiosity and in avoidance of Lena's inquiries. In the distance all he could see was flat land with miles of prairie grass, now limp and brown. According to his findings, this river valley hosted dark brown soil. Farmers near the Platte River grew mostly corn, but they also raised oats, barley, and wheat. Although Mrs. Walker's land lay farther south, he assumed the farming methods were the same. He tried to envision what fields of ripe corn looked like. From his research, he gathered tall green stalks with green shoots and a cap of brown silky-like tassels. He'd find out in the months to come.

Gabriel remembered Lena mentioning in one of her letters about a few head of cattle, but he'd neglected to find out how many or what kind. He should have asked, since he'd be working with the beasts.

A hint of excitement, a rather peculiar sensation, spread through him as he considered this adventure. For the first time in his life he'd watch things grow: corn, cattle, pigs, a garden, and two freckle-faced boys. He'd learn how to farm properly; after all, he'd read the books.

Three white-tailed deer leaped across the road from the tall grass, such wondrous creatures. My, how he admired their gracefulness. The call of a flock of geese perked his ears. Staring up into the sky, he watched their perfect V formation head south.

Winter. Philadelphia was frigid in the winter, but he'd heard Nebraska received bitter temperatures and several feet of snow, and that wasn't long in the making.

"It's all so serene," he whispered really to no one.

"Yes," Lena agreed, "but the same things making it peaceful can also turn on you if you're not careful."

"I don't believe I understand," he replied.

"Nature," she said simply. "Just when you think everything is perfect and a bit of heaven, it turns on you by throwing a twister over your land in the summer, or a prairie fire destroying everything in its path, or a blizzard to blind you in winter."

Like a beautiful woman. Gabriel studied her features beneath a faded bonnet. This time he took in the oval shape of her face and large, expressive eyes framed by nearly black hair. Her pursed lips reminded him of a rose bud. If only Lena Walker appeared a bit less lovely. Those looks could defeat a man—drive him to lose his principles. He'd seen it done too many times.

The regrets about Lena again plodded through his rambling thoughts. A plain woman whom no other man might covet had been his heart's desire. If blessed with any children, they might not look real pleasing, but he'd teach them how God examines the heart for true beauty.

Already Gabriel didn't trust Lena, and they hadn't even completed their nuptials.

three

Lena shoved a lump back down her throat. She'd made such a fool out of herself in trying to soothe Gabriel's humiliation. The laughter she'd felt for him back in Archerville had quickly turned to regret when she couldn't utter a single intelligent word.

They should be discussing the farm or arranging a time to talk about Caleb and Simon. She and Gabriel would be married in three days; they should be spending this time getting to know each other.

Fear gripped her like the time she'd sighted a cloud of grasshoppers descending on the fields ready for harvest. Gabriel Hunters was nothing like she'd pictured: He didn't look like he'd ever spent a day in his life on a farm. Well, she simply had to know the truth.

"Did you grow up on a farm?" she asked.

"Not exactly," he replied after a moment's pause.

The fright subsided to a rising anger. "Where then did you learn about it?"

"From books," he said simply, staring straight ahead.

His reply shook the very foundation on which she built her values. "From books? How can you feel the soil between your fingertips from a book? How can you tell the color of ripe wheat?"

"The written word is a valuable asset. I place complete trust in what I've read and studied." His ample chest rose and fell, while the buttons on his jacket threatened to break free. "Man has farmed since the beginning of time. If it were a difficult process, then human beings would not have survived."

I refuse to lose my temper. She clucked the horses to venture a tad faster. *I refuse to lose my temper.* "Many people have died due to crop failures or the natural hardships arising from living here. I hope you read *that* in your books."

"I have."

"And your conclusion, good sir?" She gritted her teeth to keep from adding a vicious retort.

"I have determined to be a farmer. There are many things for me to put into practice from the books I've read. If I had thought this undertaking an impossibility, I would not have answered your advertisement."

Mercy. What have I done? Lena glanced back to see Caleb and Simon still dangling their feet over the wagon. God had entrusted her with those precious boys, and she would guard them with her life. She'd see them grow to manhood and have children of their own. They needed a father—a man who had experienced life and knew its pitfalls. Somehow she doubted if Gabriel Hunters could fulfill those qualifications. She'd clearly heard God's affirmation in this strange union, but why? God must be punishing her for her pride and temper.

"Ma'am," Gabriel said just loud enough for her to hear, "I'd be grateful if you'd give me an opportunity to be the husband and father you need."

❧

Gabriel believed he had lowered himself as much as he could without some consolation in return from his future intended.

"I want to give you a chance, but you must understand how much I need a man who can work the land," Lena said, her eyes moistening.

He did not miss her tears, and immediately he wanted to whisk them away. "I will not disappoint you."

She hastily glanced away and pointed to a shadowing of buildings in the distance. "Up there is the farm. Besides the two horses, we have a mule for working the fields, a few pigs, chickens, ten cows, and a bull. Hopefully we'll have more cows in the spring."

Gabriel's first view of his new home and its outbuildings fell far below his initial ideas of a rural home. He'd seen the great farms in Pennsylvania, the clapboard homes and the well-kept barns and sheds. The conditions here ranged close to the shanty life on the poor side of Philadelphia. Bleak. Desolate.

The cabin had been constructed of sod brick made from dried prairie grass and dirt. He remembered from Lena's letter that the cabin was called a soddy. These structures kept out the heat in the summer and shut out the cold in winter. Gabriel couldn't keep from wondering if it carried a smell. However, the structure did have two windows with real paned glass.

The roof looked like the same weathered sod laid over top some type of wood. From the bare spots with shoots of plant life sprouting up from them, he assumed the roof leaked. Obviously, carpentry would be his first priority, or whatever else he deemed necessary to make the home comfortable. Using a hammer and nails shouldn't be too arduous, if those tools were required. He hadn't seen any trees, and the quandary puzzled him. Where did one find wood?

What Lena referred to as a dugout more closely resembled a cave dug out of a hillside with a portion of the front built with the same sod bricks. With his keen insight into the world of mathematics, he should be able to calculate the length and width of sod necessary for repairs. Come spring, perhaps they could locate lumber to have hauled in for a good, solid barn.

Lena pulled the wagon to a halt. The boys jumped from the back and fell into the welcoming embrace of a mangy dog that had emerged from out of nowhere. Barking and wagging its flea-bitten tail, the animal eyed the newcomer suspiciously. . .and growled.

Gabriel hesitantly stepped to the ground. He didn't care for dogs. He'd never owned one or knew anyone who did, but he'd been bitten once when he'd bent to pat a dog while walking to the Philadelphia library.

"Just let him sniff you," Caleb said, when the dog growled at Gabriel the second time. "Turnip, you need to make friends with this man. He's going to be marryin' our ma."

The dog's name is Turnip? "We don't have to do this right now," Gabriel replied as he deliberated whether to help Lena down from the wagon or wait to see if the dog took a bite from the seat of his trousers.

"Put Turnip in the barn," Lena said to her son. "Gabriel can make friends later."

Once the dog followed the boys into the dilapidated dugout, Gabriel offered her his assistance. Immediately he noticed her firm grip—stronger than his.

"You have a fine-looking place here," he said.

She frowned. "Don't add lies to your deceit. Everything is falling apart, and you know it."

"I'm not by nature an egregious person," he replied.

Lena planted her hands on her hips. "Gabe, let me tell you right now. Those big words don't mean anything to me. Here in Nebraska, we don't have time to learn the meanings of such nonsense. Using them will only upset folks, make them think you are better than they."

Is she always this petulant? And the name of Gabe? No one has ever called me anything but Gabriel.

Lena whirled away from him. He saw her shoulders rise and fall before she faced him again. "I'm sorry, Gabriel. This is not how I wanted our first meeting. We're supposed to be getting to know each other, not quarreling. Will you forgive me?"

He wondered the extent of Lena's sensibilities, for he'd certainly seen a gamut of them in the brief time they'd been together. Could he endure a lifetime of irrational emotions? Of course, he must. His mother could flare at a moment's notice, then turn her sweetness toward an unsuspecting victim. His integrity lay foremost in his mind, and he'd made a commitment to the woman before him. After all, God had given him clear direction. Hadn't He?

"I can most assuredly forgive you and take into consideration your emotions. I'd be a fool not to comprehend that my credentials do not meet with what. . .with what you anticipated. But rest assured, I will curtail my vocabulary to something more acceptable. Making good friends is important, and a proper image is quite desirable."

"Thank you, and you can start right now. I never thought I was an ignorant person, but I'm having problems following your words."

Were all women so particular? His mother had been his only example, and she always had her mind set on business—and on her disappointment in him. Lena flashed her troubled gaze his way. He could make a few concessions, since she had more to lose in this endeavor than he. "I'll do my best," he said, carefully guarding each word. "I've never been called Gabe, but it does have a pleasant sound to it."

She brightened. "You like it? Wonderful. I know Gabriel in the Bible was a messenger, and I'd like to think of you in the same way, but shortened seems to fit you."

At last she appeared happy. He inwardly sighed. Now, on to other things. "Perhaps we can talk later after your sons are in bed?"

"I'd like that very much."

He could quickly grow accustomed to Lena's smile. He offered one of his own, then quickly turned to secure his trunks from the wagon. "Where shall I put my things?"

"Inside the cabin, in the boys' room for now." She folded her hands in front of her as though searching for the courage to say something else. "I hope the barn is all right for a few days," she finally said.

"Most certainly," he replied, lifting the massive trunk into his arms. He'd ache tomorrow from this work.

"I'll fix us some supper. I hope you like venison and carrots and potatoes." When he nodded, she continued. "The boys have chores and milking to do, so we'll eat as soon as they're finished."

Gabe felt the call of a challenge. "And I'll assist the boys as soon as these are inside."

His first view of the cabin, or rather what he could see of it, astounded him. It was dark even with two windows, but the sod bricks were nearly three feet thick, which made for a wide window ledge. Lena had a few dried wild flowers setting in a crockery jug alongside a framed picture of an elderly couple.

"Your parents?" he asked, adjusting the trunk in his arms.

"Yes." She tapped her foot on the earthen floor, then pointed to a quilt near the back. "That's Caleb and Simon's room."

He maneuvered through the meagerly furnished dwelling: a rocking chair in front of a fireplace, two small benches positioned around a rough-sawn table, and two other ladder-back chairs. A small cookstove rested in the corner where a few pegs held two cast-iron pots and a skillet. Glancing about, he saw a good many household items hanging from the walls. Lena was a tidy woman. Another quilt separated the main living area from what Gabe assumed was her bedroom. He tried not to stare at it, feeling his face redden at the thought of sharing a bed with this woman. The plastered walls were a surprise to him; he'd assumed they would be covered with newspapers.

The boys' room held a chest and two straw mattresses, and he noted not much room for anything more. The earthen floor came as a shock. He'd been accustomed to wood floors with a soft rug beneath his feet. A bit of dried grass had fallen from the roof to the floor. *Surely this leaks.*

A short while later, he plodded out to the dugout, the old twinge of excitement fading to somewhat of an uncomfortable knot in the bottom of his stomach. A distinct, disagreeable smell met his nostrils. How sad, one of the boys must surely be ill.

As Gabriel entered the darkened dugout they referred to as

a barn, a horrific stench took his breath away, and he covered his nostrils. This was worse than Archerville. "Caleb, Simon, is everything all right?"

A voice replied from the shadows. "Yes, Sir. We're back here. Just starting to milk."

He recognized Caleb and ventured his way. "I'd like to help. What is that dreadful odor?"

Simon rushed down to meet him. "I don't know, 'less you're smellin' the manure."

Ah. Why didn't I detect it? "I'm sure you're right."

"It's powerful bad," Caleb said. Gabe had yet to make out the boy because his eyes were having trouble adjusting to the faint light. "Tomorrow we have to clean out this barn before Ma thrashes us."

"Perhaps I can be of assistance?" Immediately he regretted his words. Hadn't he already decided to make repairs to the various buildings?

"Oh, yes," Caleb replied, a bit too enthusiastically.

By this time, he'd made out where the young boy knelt on his knees, leaning into a brown-and-white cow. A *pinging* sound alerted Gabriel to milk squirting into the bottom of the pail. *So Caleb squeezes those conical attachments to discharge the milk.*

"When's the last time you milked a cow?" Caleb asked, grinning into his half-filled bucket.

Gabe refused to reply. "Do you have a stool?"

"He can have mine." Simon stood and peered up at him curiously. "I have one, but it's a little wobbly. Try balancing yourself with your leg."

The endeavor didn't look too difficult. He stepped over beside Simon's cow, but the stool, which was really a rickety nail keg, appeared a bit precarious. The youngest Walker bolted from his position, making room for Gabe. About that time, the cow made a woeful sound as though lamenting the milking process.

"Hush," Simon ordered. "And don't be kicking over the bucket either."

As soon as Gabe eased onto the keg, it gave way and splattered into a mass of wood pieces and a splintered seat.

"Goodness, Mr. Hunters," Simon said. "You've gone and done it now. Ma will have a word to say about this."

"You hush, Simon," Caleb said. "He couldn't help the keg breaking with his weight and all. Ma knows the difference between an accident and an on-purpose."

God help me, Gabe silently pleaded. "Boys, I can milk this cow in short order as soon as we can find a suitable stool for me."

"Ain't none," Simon said. "You'll have to bend down on your knees."

Gracious, is anything easy here? "I shall need to construct a new milking stool, but for right now I'll do as you suggest."

Gabe gingerly touched the cow. Its bristled hide felt strange, reminiscent of the short-haired dog that had bit him years ago. He wondered if cows bit.

No matter. He'd see this task to the end. All of a sudden, the appendages hanging from under the cow's belly looked rather formidable. Did he grab them one at a time or use both hands? Rubbing his fingers together, he realized the time had come to show his initiative. He reached out and grabbed an udder. It felt soft. Not at all like he'd imagined. Gabe squeezed it, and a stream of milk splattered his jacket.

"In the bucket, Mr. Hunters," Simon said impatiently. "Ma says waste not, want not."

"And she's so right," Gabe replied. "I'll not be shirking in my duties." His next attempt sent the milk into the pail. He sensed such satisfaction, but the twisted position of his body made it difficult to breathe.

"I bet you never did this before either," Lena said, towering over him.

four

Somehow Lena restrained the doubts and ugly retorts threatening to spill out over supper. Ever since she'd entered the barn with the suspicion that Gabe Hunters knew nothing about milking and discovered she was right, her mind had shaken with anger.

How had he lived for over thirty-six years without learning the basics of life? Even city folks had to eat and survive. No matter if God had been involved with this husband mess she'd gotten herself into, come morning she'd be sending Mr. Gabe Hunters packing.

To make matters worse, she'd told Caleb and Simon to clean out the barn three days ago. The smell would make a person throw up their shoes. Lena tilted her head thoughtfully. After a night in the barn, Gabe would be more than willing to leave.

"Good food, Mama," Caleb said, breaking the silence.

The fire crackled, providing all the sound Lena needed while she ate. "Thank you. Most times we have cornbread, beans, and sorghum molasses," she added in explanation to their guest. "Tonight was. . .supposed to be special. In the morning—"

"We'll get right on cleaning the barn after we deliver the milk," Gabe announced.

Lena said nothing. She had learned a long time ago about letting her temper simmer rather than letting it boil over. That method didn't always work, but tonight, laced with prayer, her angry, racing thoughts were subsiding.

"I agree with Caleb," Gabe continued. "The food is delicious."

"Thank you, Mr. Hunters." She didn't dare lift her gaze to meet his for fear she'd give into temptation and tell him just exactly what she thought about his book learning. Maybe it was enough to know he had the company of animals tonight.

"When did you want to hold our discussion?" he asked, taking a big gulp of coffee.

She swallowed a piece of molasses-soaked cornbread. "As soon as the boys go to bed. Normally, we have Bible reading before their prayers."

"May I do the honors of reading tonight and conducting prayers?"

You're going to need it by the time I'm finished with you. She bit her tongue and tried to respond civilly. "Sounds like an excellent idea. I look forward to what you'll be selecting."

"What have you been reading?"

"Job," she said.

"Mama, I don't think Mr. Hunters wants to read about a man who had sores all over his body and his family died," Caleb said. Upon meeting her scrutiny, he quickly added, "Of course, what he reads from the Bible is his choice."

"Job is fine," Gabe said. "There's something for us to learn in every piece of Scripture."

Lena glanced at his barely touched food. From the looks of him, Gabe seldom refused a meal. She lifted her coffee cup to her lips. She hadn't much of an appetite either—too many emotions floating in and out of her mind. Feeling Gabe studying her, she lifted her gaze to meet his. Kindness poured from those coppery pools and along with it a sensation akin to hurt and desperation. Her father had given her a cat once that looked at her in the same way. The animal had been beaten and left to fend for itself until her father brought it home.

A smile tugged at Lena's lips. After all, she could be kind and show him Christian hospitality until she told him there wouldn't be a wedding.

To her surprise, Gabe suggested all of them help Lena clean up from supper. Soon the dishes were washed and the debris that had fallen through the roof whisked away from the floor. A moment later, he disappeared into the boys' room and returned with spectacles in his hand.

"Here's the Bible," Lena said, handing him James's weathered book with its turned-down pages. Someday she'd give it to Caleb. All of a sudden, she wanted to jerk it back. This man had no right to take James's chair for Bible reading. She choked back a sob. "We sit by the fire, and I read from the rocking chair."

"You have to be real careful," Simon said, finding his position on a braided rug. "If you don't say the words right, the devil will pounce on you while you're in bed."

"Simon," Lena scolded. "Where ever did you hear such a thing?"

He glanced at his older brother in one giant accusing glare.

Gabe chuckled, surprising her. "Well, Simon, I haven't been able to do much since I arrived here with any expertise, but I *can* read. And the devil doesn't come after you when you're sleeping just because you can't pronounce a word correctly."

Caleb found his spot near his brother and said nothing. Lena would deal with her older son later. The two boys faced Gabe, warming their backs against the fire. If Lena hadn't been so upset, she'd have treasured the sight of her precious sons looking to a man for Scripture reading. She pulled a chair from the table, hoping he hadn't lied about knowing the Bible.

"We're near the end of Job," Lena said. "I have it marked. Oh, it's the last chapter."

Gabe carefully put on his spectacles and cleared his throat. "Job, chapter forty-two. 'Then Job answered the Lord, and said, I know that Thou canst do every thing, and that no thought can be withholden from Thee.' "

Lena felt a knocking at her heart. *I know You can do every thing, and that no thought can be kept secret from You.* She shifted uncomfortably. *Lord, I do know You are all powerful.*

Gabe continued. " 'Who is he that hideth counsel without knowledge? Therefore have I uttered that I understood not; things too wonderful for me, which I knew not.' "

This is about Gabe, isn't it? Lena knew in an instant her belittling thoughts about him had not honored God, especially when she'd doubted the Father's hand in Gabe's coming to Nebraska. She didn't understand any of it.

But he doesn't know a thing about farming. Having him around and having to teach him will be like having another child underfoot.

Lena fidgeted; the sweltering realization of being under conviction brought color to her cheeks. She glanced Gabe's way, his reading perfect against the stillness around them. Even if she had to show him how to farm, how ever would she get used to looking at him? She peered into the fire. James had presented a striking pose, and his hearty laughter had brought music to her soul. But Gabe? Although he had nice eyes, she'd have to look at his portly body and pallid skin for the rest of her life.

" 'Wherefore I abhor myself, and repent in dust and ashes.' "

Lena wanted to scream. *All right, Lord.* She wouldn't tell Gabe he had to leave. She'd teach him how to farm and tend to animals. She swallowed and choked on her own spittle, causing Gabe to halt his reading until she was all right. Yes, she'd marry him. But for the life of her, she didn't understand why, except God had ordained it, and He had a plan.

"What do you boys think about Job's life?" Gabe asked once he'd finished reading.

Simon balanced his chin on his finger. "Hmm. Pick better friends?"

Gabe smiled and ruffled his dark hair. "That's one thing. Caleb?"

"I'm not sure, Mr. Hunters. I think we're not supposed to get mad at God when bad things happen."

"Yeah," Simon piped in. "The devil might be out looking for someone to hurt and give you a wife who wants you to die."

Lena hoped the warmth in her face didn't show. Her whimsical son always saw things in a different light, and he wasn't afraid to voice his feelings.

"You're both right," Gabe said. "We don't always understand why things happen, but we can always trust that our God is in control."

Lord, You've already made me feel awful. There's no need to do it again. "Gabe, would you lead us in prayer?" she asked, hoping he didn't hear the turmoil in her voice.

He nodded. "Father God, thank You for bringing me here to this fine home. Bless Lena, Caleb, and Simon. Guide them in Your infinite wisdom and keep them safe in the shelter of Your almighty arms. Amen."

"Amen," Caleb and Simon echoed. They glanced at Lena expectantly. When she nodded, they bid Gabe good night and followed her to their small bedroom behind a blanketed curtain.

All the while she tucked them in and planted kisses on their cheeks, Lena considered the man sitting by the fireplace. She'd made a commitment to God. Now, she had to echo that same promise to Gabe.

She'd rather plow her land without a horse.

❧

Gabe twiddled his thumbs while he awaited Lena's return. He felt certain his heart would leap from his chest. What a fool he'd been to think he might belong here. Would she simply order him off her farm or tell him sweetly to take his fancy words and books back to Philadelphia? Not that he considered either request in poor taste. All his life he'd been labeled a failure, and circumstances were not about to change overnight. Learning new things and fitting into a family would take weeks, even months. Today, he'd ruined every opportune second he'd been given.

What now? *Lord, I wanted this to work. I could have learned how to farm and help Lena with those boys. I know she's not what I envisioned, but I don't think I'm what she expected either. I could have put my despicable past behind me and found confidence in being a husband and father. Oh, I know my confidence is in You, but is it a sin to desire a loving family?*

Turnip growled. Another member of the family against him. "You want to send me back on the next train too?" he whispered. He stared at the dog, trying to initiate some semblance of friendship with the mongrel.

The dog turned its mammoth head as though attempting to understand the man creature before him.

"We could have pleasant times together," Gabe continued, momentarily shoving aside his current disturbing situation with the members of this household. "Why don't you sniff at me a bit? I need a faithful companion."

Turnip focused his attention on the fire. Perhaps he contemplated Gabe's dismal mood. At least the dog wasn't growling.

"Gabe?" Lena asked quietly, interrupting his thoughts. "Would you like another cup of coffee while we talk?" She wrung her hands and offered a shaky smile.

"I'd like that very much."

"With milk?"

"I believe milk is just fine."

She felt her insides flutter while she poured the hot brew into a tin cup. "I guess we have much to talk about."

Gabe raised his hand. "Lena, I know I've failed miserably today, and I surely understand your aversion to me. I'm riddled with compunction. Let me simplify the matter. I'll leave in the morning, but I need to trouble you for a ride into Archerville."

"What is compunction?"

"It means I feel guilty and ashamed for building up your hopes, then disappointing you."

She inhaled sharply. "No. . .I'd rather you stay. . .and we follow through with our original plan."

"To marry? After I deceived you?"

She handed the coffee to him and slipped into the chair beside him. "I'm sure I have disappointed you."

Only that you are lovely. "You are exactly what God intended for me. God does not issue unfitting gifts."

His reply must have moved her, for her eyes moistened. "What sweet words. I must admit I had my doubts until you read from the Bible, but now I am sure we should marry as God put into both of our hearts—unless you have changed your mind."

He leaned forward in the rocking chair. "No, Ma'am. I came here to marry and help you, and that is what I still need to do."

She stared into the fire, and he turned his attention to the flames devouring a cow chip. Silence invaded the empty space between them.

"The preacher is expecting us day after tomorrow," Lena said quietly.

"I'll be ready."

Silence once again reigned around them.

"Caleb and Simon want to know what to call you," she finally said.

Gabe had pondered this ever since he boarded the train in Philadelphia. "I believe for now, I'd like them to call me Gabe. When and if they ever feel comfortable, they can call me something more endearing."

"Like Pa or Papa," she finished for him.

He smiled. "Yes. Our arrangement is not unusual, but I want Caleb and Simon to feel some sort of affection before choosing a fatherly title."

Again, Lena appeared moved as she brushed a tear from each cheek. "I'm pleased, Gabe."

He felt his heart lifting from his chest. "Now, I must seal our relationship properly." He slid to the front of the rocker and dropped to one knee in front of her. The effort caused him to take a deep breath. "Lena Walker, would you do me the honor of accepting my proposal of marriage? I promise to cherish you for as long as I live and to always consider Caleb and Simon as my sons." His heart softened as tears flowed more freely from her eyes. He prayed they were not shed in sadness, but in hope for a blessed future together. "I have much to learn, and I will always do my best."

Lena bit into her lower lip and smiled. "Yes, I will marry you."

five

Gabe slowly moved toward the barn, or rather the dugout, dreading the night before him. The thought gave a whole new perspective on cave dwellers. He carried a kerosene lantern in one hand and two quilts in the other, but the darkness didn't bother him, just the smell permeating the air.

"Why don't you let me make a pallet by the fire?" Lena had suggested just before he stepped out into the night. "I hate for you to sleep in the barn. The odor gags me, and I'm used to it."

"No. It simply wouldn't be appropriate. I refuse to cast any doubt upon your name. The barn will suit me until we're married."

Glancing up at a clear, star-studded night, he shoved away the unpleasantness of the sleeping arrangements by focusing on the various star formations. As a child, he'd studied them while he waited for his mother to come home. Usually he fell asleep before she stumbled in.

"Gabe," Lena called.

He turned to see her slight frame silhouetted in the doorway. The fire behind her filled his senses with a picturesque scene. An unexpected exhilaration raced up his spine. This woman would soon be his wife, and she'd been given the opportunity to negate the agreement. Maybe not all lovely women were the same. Maybe he'd been given another chance to make his life amount to something worthwhile.

"Gabe?" she called again. "No one will ever know you slept by the fire."

"I'll know," he replied, then waved. "Good night, Lena.

Tomorrow I'll help the boys clean out the barn."

He whirled around, feeling a bit giddy. For one night, he could endure most anything. Then the smell violated his nostrils like a hot furnace. What manner of insects crawled in the hay? Would the animals bother him? It would be a long night.

🍂

"All right, boys," Gabe said the following morning at breakfast. "We have a full day of work ahead of us, but I understand you have milk to deliver first."

"Yes, Sir," Caleb replied, reaching for a piece of cornbread.

"We share our milk with Mr. Shafer and his six children," Lena added. "He doesn't own a cow, and I promised his wife before she died that I would keep an eye on the children."

How commendable. "All right," Gabe said, turning back to the boys. "I'll go with you if your mother doesn't mind."

He glanced at Lena, whose pallor had turned ghastly white. "You might not want to go to the Shafers. Dagget is not the sociable type."

"Mama threw him off our land 'cause he got mad when she wouldn't marry him," Simon said. "He don't like us much, but the others are friendly."

"Simon," she uttered, her face reflecting the humiliation she must have felt. "Son, can't you ever leave well enough alone?" She stared into Gabe's face. "I feel sorry for his children since their mother died. The oldest girl, Amanda, has her hands full taking care of her brothers and sisters and dealing with her father. Caleb and Simon take the extra milk, but I don't ride along, and I don't think you would want to either."

Gabe had seen the surly type before; he'd go another day. "I'll take your advice and get started on the barn while they're gone."

Lena sighed. "I'll help until they get back. It's a nasty job." She gave the boys a stern look. "And it will never get this dirty again. Right, boys?"

"Yes, Ma'am," they chorused.

Gabe hadn't slept a wink last night, but he'd never admit it. Every time he moved, the broken ends of what little fresh hay he'd found jabbed his body like tiny needles. Before daybreak he'd nearly jumped through the roof when a rooster crowed his morning call right beside him. Then he'd discovered some sort of bites all over him. He didn't want to think what might have caused them. Although the manure smell curdled his stomach, the unaccustomed sounds of the animals—both inside and out—had also kept him awake. He'd have to ask the boys about the birds and animals in the area and how to recognize their calls. The possibility that the animals were predators flashed as a warning across his mind, not that he believed himself a fearful man, merely cautious.

In the morning light, he'd seen the structure housing the animals not only needed repairs but also existed in an overall sad state of disarray. How did they locate anything without designated areas set aside for tools, feed, harnesses, and such? This project would take more than one day, but he wouldn't be working on it tomorrow. That was his wedding day.

He glanced down at his newly purchased working clothes, thinking he should have obtained another set in Philadelphia. By tonight he'd be emitting the same stench as those animal droppings. With a shrug, Gabe headed outside, eager to begin his first day as a Nebraska farmer.

Lena took extra pains to prepare a hearty meal the morning of her and Gabe's wedding day. She hadn't slept the night before due to the anxiety about the day swirling around in her head.

"I don't believe I've had such a delectable breakfast," Gabe said.

His clothes were wet. Surely he had not tried to wash them last night.

"Lena, your cooking certainly pleases the palate. Thank you. I apologize for not complimenting you sooner."

Simon eyed Gabe curiously. "How can a pallet please you? I'd rather sleep in my bed."

Lena turned her head to keep from laughing.

"Palate, p-a-l-a-t-e," Gabe said slowly, giving the boy his utmost attention. "It means your mother's food tastes good. A pallet on the floor is p-a-l-l-e-t. It's a common mistake, because the words sound the same but are spelled differently."

Simon shook his head. "Sure can stir up strange things in a person's head. Whoever came up with words should have thought about what he was doing."

Gabe smiled. "I believe you have a valid point." He turned to Lena. "Caleb said he and Simon haven't attended school since last spring." He scooped a forkful of eggs and bacon into his mouth, then bit into a hot piece of cornbread oozing with butter.

"The schoolteacher quit after the spring session, and Archerville hasn't been able to find another," Lena replied. "I try to teach them reading, writing, and some arithmetic, but they really need someone more educated than I. I know we were lucky to have a teacher when other farms farther out have nothing."

He reached for his mug of coffee. "I'd be honored to assist in Caleb and Simon's fundamental studies."

Lena recalled Gabe had been too tired to eat supper the night before after working all day in the barn. He'd barely made it through the Scripture reading before heading to bed. How would he find time to teach the boys?

"You're welcome to do whatever you can," she said.

"Perhaps in the evenings after our meal and before Scripture reading."

"Are you sure that won't be too much trouble?" Lena asked. "I'm thinking with you here, I should have more time to devote to their book learning."

Gabe rested his fork across his plate. "Their schooling is as important as food and shelter. I'll not neglect their education. The future of this country belongs to those who aspire to higher learning. How rewarding to someday see Caleb and Simon attending a fine university."

I'd never considered them going to college. Gabe is good for them. Thank You, Lord.

An hour later, alone in the house while the boys delivered milk and Gabe prepared for the ride into Archerville, Lena pondered the day ahead, her wedding day. She wiggled her fingers into a pair of ivory-colored gloves. At least they would hide her work-worn hands. She stared at her left hand and remembered not so long ago when her ring finger was encircled by a wedding band. Only when Gabe had informed her of his arrival date in Archerville had she removed it.

Mixed emotions still battled within her. Today she planned to marry a man she did not know or love. At least she knew James before they wed. A lacing of fear caused her to tremble. Although she believed God's hand was in this marriage, she still felt like a scared rabbit.

Smoothing her Sunday, cornflower blue dress, she examined her appearance in the small mirror above her dresser. She pulled on a few wispy curls around her face, then pinched her cheeks. Inside her pocket, she'd already placed a few mint leaves to chew before the ceremony so her breath would be sweet for her wedding kiss.

A slow blush crept up her neck and face, and a chill caused her to massage her arms. She felt sordid, as though remarrying meant she no longer valued her vows to James. But that wasn't true. He would have wanted her to remarry a good man. James had been so handsome—tall, darkly tanned, muscular, and he always made her laugh. An image of Gabe flashed across her mind: his fleshy stature, the wiry straw-colored hair, and his pale skin. How could she ever learn to love and respect him? He knew nothing about living on a farm, and she questioned if he knew anything about marriage.

Yesterday, with the boys, he'd cleaned out the entire barn and organized tools and equipment, which hadn't been done since before James's illness and not ever to the extent of Gabe's high standards. He'd planned on Friday, the day after their wedding, to build another milk stool and make roof repairs to the barn. The stool would have to wait, since lumber was too dear. Gabe had looked happy, satisfied with what he'd accomplished. She felt relieved about this part of him. Goodness knows what she'd have done if he'd been a lazy sort.

"We want to call Mr. Hunters, Gabe," Caleb had announced. "I'm not so sure he knows how to be a father. Why, Mama, I had to tell him what some of the tools were used for."

Oh, Lord, I know You are in this. Help me to be a good wife and not compare Gabe to James. Hold onto my tongue and help me to be sweet-tempered.

Lena heard the door to the soddy open. "Mama," Caleb called. "It's time to go."

six

"Kindly take the bride's right hand," the Reverend Jason Mercer instructed. He towered over Gabe as he cleared his throat and continued with the wedding ceremony. "Repeat after me."

Although he shook with thoughts of the future, Gabe repeated the vows word for word. "I, Gabriel Hunters, take thee, Lena Walker, to be my wedded wife, to have and to hold from this day forward, for better or for worse, for richer or for poorer, in sickness and in health, to love and to cherish, till death us do part, according to God's holy ordinance; and thereto I plight thee my troth." Nervousness tore at his whole heart and mind—to say nothing for what it was doing to his body. He stared into Lena's incredible green eyes and saw the same trepidation.

Poor lady, she'd said little on the ride here, and now her hand trembled like a fall leaf shaking loose from a mighty tree. How arduous this must be for her.

Standing alone in the church except for his soon-to-be family, the reverend, and a friend of Lena's, Nettie Franklin, Gabe appreciated that no one else gawked at them. He desperately needed solace.

"Repeat after me, Lena," the reverend said.

"I, Lena Walker, take thee, Gabriel Hunters, to be my wedded husband, to have and to hold from this day forward, for better or for worse, for richer or for poorer, in sickness and in health, to love and to cherish, till death us do part, according to God's holy ordinance; and thereto I plight thee my troth." Her voice quivered. Gabe held her hand firmly, understanding

45

her fears for the day and tomorrow because he had just as many if not more. Only God could ease their uncertainty.

"Do you have a token of love?" Reverend Mercer asked.

"Yes, Sir," Gabe replied in a voice not his own. He reached into his jacket pocket and pulled out his mother's ring, a striking red ruby set in gold, not gaudy but dainty and elegant. It had been the only thing he'd kept of her possessions, because it once belonged to his great-grandmother.

As they joined their right hands, Gabe held his breath until he slipped the heirloom onto her left ring finger. *Thank You, Lord, for allowing Mother's ring to fit.* She'd left him something of value after all.

Behind Lena, Caleb and Simon stood solemn. No doubt Caleb, acting on behalf of the family, had misgivings about Gabe's qualifications as a provider. These first two days had been such a disappointment, and Gabe had to ask the boys about everything. He looked like a simpleton.

The two youngsters stared at him in a mixture of disbelief and confusion. From the looks of them—thick, mottled brown hair and wide, dark eyes—Lena's deceased husband must have been a dandy. Now, she had a man who held the same shape as a pot-bellied stove—painted white.

"By the power vested in me, I pronounce you Man and Wife. What God hath joined together, let no man put asunder." The kindly young reverend paused and smiled. "You may now kiss your bride."

I've never kissed a woman before. How am I supposed to do this? Should I have rehearsed or found a book?

Gabe stepped closer, his bulging midsection brushing against Lena's waist. He lightly grasped her thin shoulders and bent ever so slightly. She quivered with his touch, and he prayed it was not from aversion. Her lovely features settled on him in a most pleasing manner, reminding him of an angel depicted in a stain-glassed window at his church in

Philadelphia. To him, Lena had given beauty its name. Maybe God had given him a woman he could trust after all.

"Thank you, Lena, for giving this lowly man your hand," he whispered.

Tears graced her eyes, and he seized the moment to offer a feathery kiss to her lips. "I am most honored."

The seal of their commitment, Gabe's first kiss, tasted warm and sweet with a hint of mint. Quite agreeable. In fact, he could easily grow accustomed to this endearment.

"Congratulations," Reverend Mercer said in a booming voice. Over the few years he'd served as clergy, the reverend must have repeated a thousand "amens," but none as meaningful as the one Gabe interpreted as a blessing upon this ceremony.

"Thank you," Lena said quietly to the reverend.

Nettie, a pleasant-looking young woman, reached out to hug Lena. "I'll be praying for you every day," she said.

The two women's eyes flooded with tears. "Don't make me cry. This is a happy occasion," Lena said, dabbing at her eyes.

"Yes, it is, and you deserve all the good things God can give," Nettie replied, offering a smile.

Gabe offered Nettie his hand in a gesture of friendship. "Thank you for witnessing the ceremony. I'm grateful."

"I'm sure you will be very happy," the reverend continued with a nod. For a young man, his hair had rapidly escaped its original seating. He grasped Gabe's hand. "I have a good feeling you will make a splendid husband and a fine father."

"I don't know about that, Reverend Mercer," Simon said with a deep sigh. "Mr. Gabe needs to learn some farmin' and how to ride a horse first."

Gabe glanced into the little boy's face, seriousness etched on his features. How should he respond when the boy spoke the truth?

Lena whirled around to face her youngest son. "Simon, you apologize this instant." She met Gabe's gaze. Her face had transformed from ashen to crimson in a matter of a few moments. "I am so sorry. I'll properly discipline him when we get home."

"No need," Gabe said as gently as possible. This was his family, and he needed to take control but not exhibit harsh or domineering ways. "I have a better idea, if you don't mind."

When Lena said nothing, he lowered to one knee and eyed Simon. "No one knows more than this man before you all the items I need to learn and experience, but you could have voiced your concerns in a more mannerly fashion. So, while you are feeding the animals this afternoon by yourself, Caleb will be teaching me the fine art of bridling, saddling, and riding a horse. When you're finished, you can offer any helpful advice."

Simon's eyes widened, and Caleb muffled a snicker. "Yes. . .Sir."

"Good." Gabe stood and caught a glint of admiration in Lena's eyes. "Is this suitable?" he asked her.

"Most definitely." Lena smiled, and his heart turned a flip.

Oh, Lord, help me to be worthy of this woman. If only she weren't so comely. Ignoring the misgivings pouring through his mind, Gabe offered her his arm. "Mrs. Hunters, may I escort you to our carriage? I will then take care of the monetary arrangements with the good reverend and drive you home, with your careful instructions of course." He shot a glance at Caleb and Simon, who thankfully chose to say nothing.

She linked her arm with his. Her touch exhilarated his spirit. *I'm a married man, and I have two sons!*

❧

Lena listened to the sounds of her son's laughter coming from the barn while she lowered the bucket into the well. She caught sight of the ruby ring, thinking once more how beautiful its brilliance and how out of place the ring looked on her weather-beaten hand. Gabe's mother must have been a highly educated and sophisticated woman.

"Mama," Caleb called from the barn.

She turned to see Gabe riding the mare toward her with no assistance. He sat erect in the saddle, and his hands held the reins firmly. Without his hat, the late afternoon sun over his shoulder picked up the pale blond of his hair, reminding her of ripe corn. *Gabe Hunters, I believe with a little physical work and the sun to darken your skin, you just might strike a fine pose.*

Immediately she detested her impetuous thoughts. The Bible clearly stated the measure of a man dwelled in his heart, not in his looks.

"How quickly you learn," she said, drawing up the water and setting the bucket aside.

"I believe my ability to progress is due to Caleb's excellent instructions," Gabe replied. He'd pulled the mare to a halt and talked to her while leaning from the saddle.

Crossing her arms, she laughed. "Mr. Hunters, you do catch on fast. Why you look like you were born in a saddle."

Gabe joined in her laughter. "We'll discuss my riding ability after I learn how to trot and gallop. Perhaps in time we could ride together."

"It's been a long while since I've enjoyed riding," she said wistfully. An image of her and James riding across the plains so many years ago flew across her mind.

He dismounted, a bit clumsily, but successfully. "You work too hard," he said, grasping the reins in one hand and picking up the bucket in the other.

"That's life on a farm," she said simply. His nearness served to remind her of the vows they'd shared earlier in the day. For a moment she'd forgotten, not really wanting to think about it all. Then she remembered the night and her wifely duties. . . . The unknown had always been frightening, and although farm life seemed insurmountable before, now she had a husband who knew less about toiling the land than her sons.

"I want to do all I can to make your land profitable."

His words sounded as though he'd read her thoughts. "Thank you." She glanced again at her left hand. "My ring is far above anything I've ever owned," she murmured. "Is it a family heirloom?"

"My great-grandmother's passed to my mother." He smiled. "I'm glad you're pleased."

"I've never owned anything so fine."

"It reminds me of you and the thirty-first chapter of Proverbs. 'Who can find a virtuous woman? For her price is far above rubies.' "

Lena felt the tears spill swiftly over her cheeks. The precious gems flowing from Gabe's mouth came so natural. His words touched her heart with a special warmth and beauty of their own. *Must be from his books, and I can barely keep up with the boys' schoolwork.*

"Have I upset you?" he asked, his strawlike eyebrows knit together.

"No." She shook her head. How could she tell him, this stranger—her husband—all the fears, doubts, and questions racing through her mind about him and this ruse of a marriage?

She'd entered into this with only thoughts of herself. She'd wanted a farmhand and a model for her sons. Not once had she considered this person might have feelings and emotions. The very thought he might be sensitive with the potential of caring very deeply for a new family never had really occurred to her.

I am so selfish. Gabe doesn't deserve a woman like me. Rubies? Lena thought the verse about throwing pearls to swine best befit her.

"Lena," he whispered.

She knew her eyes held her turmoil when she should be happy this first afternoon of their marriage. Unbidden droplets of liquid pain coursed down her cheeks.

"I think it best if I continue to sleep in the barn."

"Why?" Had she hurt him so badly he could not bear being with her?

Gabe moistened his lips. She'd learned in the three short days they'd been together that he often did this before he spoke of important matters. "We do not know each other, and of utmost importance is for us to be friends." He cleared his throat. "Affection should be present before we live as man and wife, don't you think? And how else can we develop a fondness for each other unless we first appreciate our strengths and talents?"

Oh, Lord, is Gabe a saint or simply terribly wounded by my initial reaction to him?

❧

She detests me. My inadequacies have destroyed any hope of respect. Gabe wanted to place a hand on her shoulder, but he dared not see her recoil. Lena's tears moved him so deeply he feared if he didn't turn away, he too might weep.

All of his doubts about her beauty and possible unfaithfulness surfaced and drowned in his inward grief. He had spoiled what could have been great joy. In all of his grandiose ideas of learning to live on a farm and all it entailed, why had he foolhardily thought he could experience the knowledge by reading books? Now, the theory burst in his face. As his mother always said, "Gabriel, you are an utter disappointment. I can't love anyone who is such a fool. Live your life in your books; see where it gets you. Nowhere, I tell you. Nowhere."

"I want what you want," Lena said, between sobs. "If this is how you believe our lives should begin, then so be it." She lifted her tear-glazed face. "Perhaps we should have corresponded more before your trip here."

Gabe felt his heart plummet. If they had written numerous letters, she would have detected his deception. "I'm sorry for allowing you to believe I knew about farming and living by the sweat of my brow. But I will learn—"

"I know you will," she interrupted, taking the bucket of water from his hand. She paused, staring at the water as though it offered the answers to the dilemma plaguing them. "Do you want to leave?"

Gabe refused to answer, carefully forming his words. He took in a panoramic view of the farm—the work it needed, the work he didn't know how to do. He should give her and the boys an escape from the community's ridicule. They need not be the victims of his idiocy. Defeat wrapped a black hand around his heart and strangled the utterances he believed proper and fitting for the situation.

"No, Lena, I don't want to leave. I came here to start a new life, and I want to stay."

seven

Lena marched down the front of Archerville's Gospel Church, where only four days earlier she and Gabe had spoken their vows. Nervousness had attacked her then, but not as much as the sense of every eye in the building studying her and Gabe now. What a sight they must present—Lena shivering like a new bride, her husband carrying his traveling hat with his wild hair and filled-up suit, and her barefoot sons pretending they weren't embarrassed by it all. To make matters worse, Riley O'Connor sat on the aisle seat midway down.

Oh, Lord, I'm so sorry, but I feel like the whole church is laughing at me. She glanced at her new husband and offered him a shaky smile. Gabe might not give the appearance of a Nebraska farmer, but he certainly had treated her and the boys well. Unless something changed, he was a giving man and anxious to learn about farming. But those resolves didn't help her face the forty people attending this Sunday morning service.

"Good morning," Amanda Shafer whispered. Unlike her father, Dagget, Amanda was a sweet, pretty sixteen-year-old who loved the Lord and took the best possible care—under the circumstances—of her brothers and sisters.

"Mornin'." Lena hooked her arm into Gabe's. "Amanda, this is my husband, Gabriel Hunters. Gabe, this is Amanda Shafer."

"A pleasure to make your acquaintance, Miss Shafer," Gabe said, his every word pronounced perfectly. . .and sounding foreign. "Or is it missus?"

"Miss," Amanda replied. "And these are my brothers and sisters."

53

After Amanda politely introduced her siblings, she added, "We're neighbors and see Caleb and Simon 'most every day."

"Amanda is a big help to her pa in raising these children," Lena hastily added, eyeing an empty pew two rows up from where they stood.

"Your father must be very proud of you. Is he here that I might introduce myself?"

Amanda's face flushed pink. "No, Pa is at home today."

He needs to be here with his family.

Reverend Mercer greeted Lena and Gabe as he made his way down to the front of the sod-bricked church. Thankful for the interruption, Lena urged her family to the empty bench near the front. At least there she wouldn't have to endure the stares from the rest of the congregation.

Lena attempted to concentrate on the sermon, but the topic caused her to cringe from the moment Reverend Mercer read from the Bible about God looking at a man's heart rather than his physical appearance. *All right, Lord. You shamed me, and I know You're right.* Sitting up straighter, she patted Gabe's arm and focused her gaze on Reverend Mercer, although her ears didn't take in another word.

At the close, Reverend Mercer stood before his small congregation and teetered back and forth on his heels. "I have an announcement to make. This past week I had the pleasure of marrying Lena Walker and Gabriel Hunters. Let's all take a moment to congratulate this fine couple. Mr. Hunters is from Philadelphia and welcomes the task of farming in our fine country." He motioned for Gabe and Lena to stand and face the people. Slapping on a smile, she nodded at the well-wishers and ignored the snickers. Caleb and Simon stared straight ahead at the door, and she wished she could do the same.

"Mr. and Mrs. Hunters, would you and the boys kindly join me in the back so each one of these fine people can greet you?"

Oh, no. Dagget may not be here, but Riley O'Connor is. Knowing that man's quick tongue, he's liable to say anything after I refused his improper advances. Sure glad I walloped him when I could. Instantly, Lena felt sorry for Gabe. He'd be caught like a snared rabbit, unsuspecting in the least of Riley's insults.

৯

Gabe greeted each face with a smile. He appreciated the sincere welcomes from most of the people and their desire to be friends. But he also saw the wary expressions and mocking stares from a few. How well he knew the judgmental type, whether they lived in Archerville, Nebraska, or Philadelphia, Pennsylvania. If you didn't wear the clothes they wore, converse in their familiar words, or come from an acceptable family, then you were cast at the bottom of their list. He'd seen it too long and well recognized the characteristics.

Fortunately, he had an opportunity to prove himself capable and responsible to those who mattered—Lena and her sons. God valued him and had given him the distinction of being a part of this community. By His hand, he'd succeed.

"Good to have you here," a wrinkled elderly lady said after stating her name. She patted his hand and gave a toothless smile. Slivers of gray peeked beneath her bonnet. "Lena is a fine woman, strong and determined."

"Thank you, Ma'am. We'll be happy, I'm sure."

"Pure pleasure to meet you. Glad you're here," a balding man said. Dressed in a little better attire than most folks there, he introduced himself as Judge Hoover. "I'd like for you to meet my wife, Bertha." A round woman smiled prettily, but before Gabe could respond, the judge continued. "This is a growing town, and I praise God for each newcomer." He swung his arm around Reverend Mercer's shoulders and ushered him outside into the fall sunlight with his quiet wife behind him.

Then Gabe met the eyes of a tall, slender fellow who eyed him contemptuously. "Hunters, eh?" He kept both hands on a tattered hat in front of him. "Sure don't look like a farmer to me. Ya won't last here."

Remember, Sir, we are in God's house. Gabe had dealt with this type of person longer than he cared to remember. "Looks are often deceiving, as the reverend so eloquently established this morning," Gabe said. "The good Lord willing, I will succeed at my endeavors."

If the ill-mannered man could have spit in church, Gabe surmised he'd have done so. Furrowing his brow, the fellow turned his attention to Lena. Immediately, he became charming in every sense of the word.

"Lena." His words dripped with honey. "You look right pretty this morning." He smiled broadly, revealing a row of perfectly white teeth—not a common sight, and certainly an edge to any man wishing to impress a woman.

Gabe ran his tongue over his own teeth—fairly straight and not discolored from tobacco. *Have you forgotten she is my wife?*

Lena lifted her chin and glanced at the door. "Riley O'Connor, your horse is waiting for you."

"How soon before you get bored with this city feller?" he asked just loud enough for Gabe to hear. Leaning a little closer to the new Mrs. Hunters than Gabe deemed proper, Riley turned to Gabe and sneered. "She never minded my kisses. In fact she asked for more."

Lena lifted her hand as if she might strike him.

"It's all right, Lena," Gabe soothed, not once taking his gaze from Riley. He feared she was ready to unleash her temper, not that he wouldn't enjoy seeing this rude fellow with freshly slapped cheeks, but God didn't ordain this type of behavior and fighting as a means of settling disputes.

"Mr. O'Connor, I am currently overlooking your deficiency

of manners, but when issues pertain to my wife, I thank you kindly to refrain from indecorous speech."

Riley issued him a snarl.

"In other words, Mr. O'Connor, Lena Hunters is a married woman and does not desire to hear your crude remarks." Gabe turned to Lena. "Is that a correct assumption, Dear?"

"Yes, it is," she replied and dismissed Riley in one seething glare. A young woman carrying a baby stood behind Riley. "Martha, your little girl is growing like a weed, and look at those sky-blue eyes. Can I hold her?"

Riley stumbled down the steps in a huff and headed straight to a horse tethered beyond the wagons.

Once the receiving line for Archerville's Gospel Church had diminished, Gabe expelled a long breath. He leaned down to Caleb and whispered, "How did I do?"

Caleb pressed his lips together in an obvious gesture to suppress his mirth. "You did right well. Judge Hoover shook your hand, which means he likes you, and he can be rather bad-tempered. And. . .you put Riley in his place."

"Thanks," Gabe replied. "I do believe I'm ready for the peace and quiet of our farm."

He glanced at Lena, whose face resembled a color somewhere between gray and flour white. *Did she and Mr. Riley O'Connor court before I came? Was his arrogance a result of being a jealous suitor?* Rolling the conversation with Riley around in his jumbled mind, Gabe could only dispel the despairing thoughts with a shiver.

"Shall we go home?" His question sounded weak.

"Please," she uttered, once again hooking her arm onto his.

Outside the sod church, Reverend Mercer lingered at the Shafer wagon while holding a little girl who hid her face in his jacket.

"Excellent sermon this morning," Gabe called to him.

The reverend turned and waved enthusiastically. "Thank

you. Mighty glad to have you with us. See you next week?"

"We'll be here," Gabe assured him.

"Has someone invited you to dinner?" Lena asked the reverend.

Are you not wanting to be alone with me. . .because of Riley?

"Yes, Ma'am."

Her shoulders relaxed. "We'd love to have you come next Sunday."

The reverend smiled and thanked her politely before handing the bashful child back to Amanda Shafer.

Seeming to ignore Gabe and Lena, Caleb and Simon chattered in the wagon, caught up in their own world of trapping animals and teasing each other.

"Are you displeased with me?" Gabe asked softly. He held both reins firmly as had been his instructions.

She gasped. "Oh, no." Shaking her head, she adjusted her sunbonnet. "I'm so sorry about what happened."

"You mean the saturated infant I was asked to hold?" He didn't want to upset her if she truly felt badly about Riley.

Her gaze flew to his, and she blinked back a tear.

Now, I've truly upset her.

"Riley O'Connor," she uttered, as though his name were a curse. "I'm so sorry for the things he said to you."

"To me? Ma'am, he insulted you."

She shrugged and stared up at the sky "He insulted both of us, Gabe. I want you to know that I never courted him. Not ever. I wouldn't allow him near me, which is probably why he was so mean today."

"You don't have to explain it to me—"

"But I want to! He asked me to marry him, and I refused. He's been like that ever since."

Another thought needled at Gabe. "Should I have challenged him outside? Did you expect me to engage him in a fistfight?"

"Goodness, no. You handled him much better than I could ever have."

When she sniffed, he yearned to extend consolation to her. "The situation is over and done. Perhaps he won't trouble you again now that we're married."

"I hope not." She forced a laugh. "I nearly blacked his eyes. Oh, I wanted to, Gabe."

Gabe laughed heartily. "I saw. I'll be sure to avoid making you angry."

And she joined him, laughing until the boys begged to know what was so funny.

eight

Lena rocked gently in front of the fireplace, enjoying its familiar creaking like an old friend. She loved these moments: quiet, peaceful times while she tended to mending. The only sounds around her came from the mantle clock's steady rhythm and the comfortable rocker. Usually Gabe taught the boys their lessons during this time and then treated them all to a chapter in some magnificent book. Nightly he read from the Scriptures and led in prayer.

Tonight, the men in her family had hurried from supper to make sure the animals were all secure. The temperature outside had dropped considerably during the afternoon, and the wind whistled about their soddy like a demon seeking entrance. Snow clouds hovered over them all day, and she knew without a doubt that the sky planned to dump several inches of snow—possibly several feet—before morning.

Inserting her needle into Caleb's torn drawers, she worked quickly to patch the knees. He'd most likely need the clothing tonight. Fall had passed with no hint of Indian summer; suddenly the warm days of early September changed to a chilling cold in October and now November. The dropping temperatures alarmed her, and she prayed the winter would be easy. Usually the frigid weather waited to besiege them until at least December, with the coldest days landing in January and February.

Lena paused and stared into the crackling fire. A smile tugged at her lips. This past month as Mrs. Gabriel Hunters had been good and ofttimes humorous. Gabe was indeed a fine husband—maybe not exactly what she wanted or envisioned—but

God knew best. Such a tenderhearted, compassionate man, but he had his unique moments. When he decided to complete a task, he refused to give in to the cold, time of day, mealtime, or lack of knowledge. Tenacious, he called it, but she knew better. Gabe had a stubborn streak as clear as she knew her name.

My, how she appreciated having her husband around. Praise God, Gabe hadn't mentioned the unfortunate incident with Riley again. Riley hadn't been back to church—for which Lena was grateful, especially given that hearing God's Word had done nothing to improve the man's disposition.

The sound of Gabe's hearty laughter and the giggles of her sons caressed her ears as if she'd been graced by the sweetest music ever sung this side of heaven.

"Mama, we're ready for a winter storm," Caleb said, once all three had made their way inside.

"I'm glad," she called from the rocking chair, smiling at her sons, then meeting a sparkle in Gabe's merry gaze. *He enjoys this work. Seems to thrive on it.*

"If you don't mind, Lena," he said, "we went over our arithmetic in the barn. So I'd like to work on our reading tonight."

"A story?" Simon asked. "When we're all done with our lessons?"

Gabe chuckled. "I imagine so, providing your reading expertise surpasses my expectations."

Caleb placed his coat on a peg by the door and turned to his younger brother. "That means we do well."

Simon crinkled his forehead. "I know what it means. I study my *vocaberry* words."

"Vocabulary," Caleb corrected. "The correct pronunciation of the English language is a declaration of our appreciation for education." He nodded at Gabe as though reciting before a schoolmaster.

Lena stifled a laugh. Caleb, who had not shown much

interest in schooling before, had blossomed under Gabe's instructions. He actually looked forward to his schoolwork.

"I don't need to know how to say words as proper as you," Simon said between clenched teeth. "I'm just going to be president of the United States, and you're going to be a doctor."

"Both are worthy callings," Gabe said. "No point in brothers becoming adversaries. Neither profession is above the other or requires less expertise. Education is vital to any man's vocation."

"Even a farmer?" Caleb asked.

"Absolutely. A farmer needs to know how and when to till the soil, take care of the animals, how to make repairs, and a host of other necessities too numerous for me to mention."

Simon shrugged and sighed heavily. "Sounds like I will be tending to my lessons until I'm an old man."

"Precisely," Gabe replied and ruffled his hair. "We never stop learning; that's why God gave us eager minds. Now, gather your slate, so you can inscribe any words for which you do not comprehend the meaning while I read."

Thank You, Lord, for directing this man to my sons. I've never heard such wisdom.

"And what will you be reading this night, providing the boys master their work?" Lena asked, not wanting Gabe to see her enthusiasm at the prospect of another exciting tale.

Gabe thrust his hands behind his back and teetered on his heels. "I think a new book, *David Copperfield*, by Charles Dickens. I believe the boys will enjoy the tale of a young boy in England and his adventures. There is much to learn about life and England in this novel."

Lena caught his gaze and a faint shimmer of something she had not felt in years swept through her. *Lord, what a blessing if I learn to love this man.*

Gabe settled in beside her on a rag rug. He'd begun teaching the boys in this manner, stating they learned more when they shared eye contact. Obviously, he was right.

"Are you weary tonight?" he asked her quietly.

Her heart hammered. Why did Gabe ask her this? "No. Is there something that needs to be done?"

"Only my hair needs to be cut before church tomorrow. It reminds me of straw, and the longer it grows, the more unruly it becomes until I look like an overstuffed scarecrow."

She calmed her rapid pulse. *Oh my. I nearly had a fright.* They still remained as friends, with Gabe sleeping in the barn. For a moment, she wondered if he'd decided to claim his rights as her husband. "I'd be glad to. Perhaps I can help you since it wants to go its own way."

"I'd be much obliging," he replied. "I've never been able to comb my hair so it would lay smoothly."

Once Caleb and Simon finished their lessons and they all heard the first chapter of *David Copperfield*, the boys scurried off to bed amidst the rising howl of the wind outside.

"I'll bring in some more chips from the porch and a few corn cobs for the cookstove," Gabe said, reaching for his coat. "You know better than I do how much snow may fall, and I want to be prepared."

"Maybe a few inches, but most likely a few feet." Lena pressed her lips together. Snow always frightened her, more so than the other threats of nature. James had become ill in this kind of weather, then died of pneumonia. "I can cut your hair when you come back inside."

A short while later, she pulled a chair beside the fire, where Turnip rested with his face in his paws. Pulling her scissors from her apron pocket and securing a comb from the bedroom, she waited for Gabe to dump an armload of chips near the dog.

Once seated, he shook his head. "Only a miracle or losing all of my hair could help."

Lena laughed lightly. "I don't think you will go bald any

time soon." She dragged a comb through his thick hair, all the while pondering its wildness and his wiry eyebrows. "Have you ever tried combing it in the direction it grows?"

"You mean straight up?"

She joined him in another laugh. "Not exactly, but do you mind if I try something?"

"Whatever you can do will be an improvement."

She touched his shoulders and felt him shudder. For certain, she hadn't been this close to him since he'd kissed her on their wedding day. "I'll do my best," she managed, remembering the shiver she'd felt with his gaze earlier. "Do you mind if I wet it a little?"

"Uh. . .well. . .certainly."

Odd, he's never been at a loss for words. Makes me wonder if something is happening between us. Lena shook her head. *Of course not, we've barely known each other a month.*

All the while she dampened Gabe's hair, she saw chill bumps rise on his neck. "I'm sorry this is cold. I used warm water."

"You're. . .you're fine," he said.

She glanced at his face—red, too red even for their position in front of the fire. *I can't stop now. What will he think?* Swallowing hard, she continued combing his hair, easing the coarse strands in the direction they wanted to go—straight back rather than to the side. The change amazed her. His face looked thinner, and his eyes seemed larger—like huge copper pennies.

"Have you not combed your hair back before? Why, it looks wonderful," she said. "I can trim it a little, but Gabe, you look positively dashing."

His face now resembled a summer's tomato. She hadn't meant to embarrass him, but he did look. . .well, striking. With a snip here and there, his hair rested evenly over his head. She couldn't help but run her fingers through the thick, blond mass. Instantly, she realized what she was doing and trembled. Whatever had she been thinking?

"Do. . .do you mind if I cut a bit of your eyebrows since they tend to stick up too?" she asked.

He shook his head and moistened his lips. *This is hard for both of us!*

Once completed, she excused herself long enough to fetch her handled mirror from her bedroom. "Just look, Gabe."

He took the mirror and their fingertips met—a gentle touch, but it seared her as though she'd stuck her hand in the midst of a hot flame.

Shakily placing the mirror in front of his face, he leaned closer. "You've worked wonders," he mumbled.

"No, I haven't. You have beautiful hair; it simply has a mind of its own."

He examined his image more closely, turning the mirror from side to side to catch every angle. "Even without a hat, it will not stick out like a porcupine."

She laughed and moved to face him. "Your hair looks good, and your face is pleasing too." *Now, why did I say that?*

"Uh, thank you, but I believe you've been isolated on this farm too long. It's affecting your judgment." He avoided her gaze, and she too felt terribly uncomfortable at her brash statements. "I think it's time I ventured to the barn."

Lena nodded, but another whistle of the wind alarmed her. "Gabe, the barn is simply too cold for you to sleep out there. Why, you'll freeze to death."

This time his ears reddened. "Nonsense. I will be snug and warm."

"I refuse for my husband to sleep in a barn when this soddy is where you belong."

He stood and strode across the room for his coat. "And I say, the barn suits me fine." He reached for the latch. "I have two warm quilts out there."

"Would you like a comforter?"

Gabe stared at her incredulously, and she grasped his interpretation in horror. "I mean a third blanket."

He hesitated. "If it will not inconvenience you."

On unsteady legs, Lena made her way to the blanket chest in her bedroom and brought him a thick new quilt. He thanked her and opened the door. An icy gust of wind hurled its fury at them.

"Please, Gabe, stay inside tonight."

"No, this is what I committed to do until we are ready to live as man and wife."

Your stubbornness will make you ill. She grabbed her coat and muffler. "Then I'm going with you."

nine

"Most certainly not!" Gabe replied, a little louder than he intended.

"If you insist upon freezing to death, I will most certainly join you," Lena replied, shrugging into her coat.

Completely frustrated, Gabe toyed with the proper words to convince her of her absurdity. He'd tried so hard to refrain from using the vocabulary that confused those around him, but his mind spun with the terms familiar to him.

"See, you cannot even argue against me." She swung her muffler around her neck and face.

"What must I do to convince you of this foolishness?" he asked with an exasperated sigh.

"Be sensible and sleep inside by the fire."

I'll agree until you fall asleep. "All right. I concede to your pleas, but I must get my quilts from the barn."

"If you aren't back in ten minutes, I'm coming out there."

Gabe nodded, speechless. He knew Lena meant every word. He lifted the chain deep inside his overalls pocket holding his pocket watch. From what he'd seen of his wife with Caleb and Simon, he dared not proceed a moment past her ultimatum.

Odd, he used to have to tug on that chain to retrieve his pocket watch. Glancing at the small clock on the fireplace mantle, he double-checked the time.

"I'll be waiting," she said, folding her hands at her waist.

He'd seen that menacing look on her face before. The lightning stare didn't occur often, but he understood the flash occurred before the thunder. Truth of the matter was, he enjoyed Lena's feisty moments. She'd told him right from the start about her temper, but he'd yet to see it vex him. The few times she lashed out at the boys, they needed an upper hand.

The frigid air nearly took his breath away—a raw-bone cold that sought to solidify his blood. Gabe buttoned his coat tighter around him. Used to be the outer garment didn't fasten. Another oddity.

Loyal Turnip braved the cold with him. "Thanks," he said to the dog. "I believe we men need to form lasting bonds." Moments later he returned with his quilts, after giving himself enough time to check on the livestock.

Once he glanced at the roaring fire, he saw she'd made a soft pallet before the burning embers. All those less than comfortable nights in the barn plodded across his mind. The smells there were still offensive, but he'd grown accustomed to them, and the sounds of animals—both inside and out—no longer jolted him from his sleep. With the cold came the likelihood of fewer insect bites.

Then he saw Lena. She'd removed her outer garments, but she'd been busy.

"What are you doing?" he asked at the sight of her constructing a second pallet beside his.

"I'm staying here beside you until you go to sleep," she replied, not once looking his way. "Gabe, you're a determined man, and as soon as you hear my even breathing in the next room, you'll be out the door and to the barn. Won't happen if I'm here. I sleep like a cat."

Have I met my match? We'll see who falls asleep first.

"And why are you so insistent about my sleeping arrangements?" He chuckled.

She wrapped her shawl about her shoulders. "The boys' father stepped out into a blizzard and caught pneumonia. Before two months passed, he'd died."

Gabe frowned. "I'm sorry, Lena, but I'm overly healthy. Just take a look at my portly size."

"If you haven't noticed, you're losing weight." Her features softened. "I don't want to lose another husband."

With elegant grace, Lena slowly descended to the floor, sitting on the rag rug where he'd taught the boys their lessons. She pulled her knees to her chest and wrapped her arms around the faded blue dress she wore every day but Sunday. An intense desire to draw her to him and kiss her soundly inched across his mind—just as it had earlier when she'd touched him. He couldn't have this. Gabe Hunters had made a commitment. He'd feign sleep, then creep to the barn.

"Shall we talk?" he asked. "I'm not ready to retire."

"I'd like that," she replied quietly. "Is there anything you need? The pillow is nice and soft."

"No, I'm fairly comfortable, thank you."

Gabe studied her, this enigma before him. This puzzling, confusing, perplexing woman who bore his name. So unlike his mother, Lena's spirit heightened with compassion and tenderness, even when angered. He didn't want to learn to love her, not really. A part of him didn't trust or rather refused to trust a woman as lovely as Lena Hunters. But. . .in quiet moments like these, he allowed himself to dream of this genteel woman loving him.

"You are an excellent teacher for the boys," she said, resting her chin on her knees. "They are learning so much."

He smiled, recalling their impish grins and eager minds. "They are teaching me as much if not more."

"We've been married a month," she said, glancing his way.

"A good month. An abundance of work has been done."

"Some days, I think you work too hard."

"Nonsense. I must compensate for all the skills I lack in farming."

She sighed, and her shoulders lifted slightly. "I'm impressed with what you've accomplished. You're making yourself into a fine farmer." With lowered lashes, she stared back at the fire. As though mesmerized by its brilliance, she blinked and took another deep breath.

She's exhausted. My poor Lena, and she's concerned about my welfare.

"You need your rest," he urged.

"I will when you fall asleep. Shall I read to you?"

He pondered her question. "I believe so, then I'll read to you."

She nodded and reached for the Bible. "What would you like to hear?"

"I don't have a preference. Why not your favorite passage?"

So close he could see a shimmer from her fire-warmed cheeks, Gabe listened to Lena read the book of Ruth. No wonder she chose this accounting of such a godly woman. Ruth, like Lena, was a widow who put her faith and trust in the Almighty God. He delivered Ruth from her poverty and blessed her in the lineage of Jesus Christ. How wonderful if Gabe could be Lena's blessing.

He listened to every word, concentrating on the musical lilt of her voice. She was tiring; too many times she shifted and straightened to stay awake.

"No matter how many times I hear Ruth's story, I'm impressed with her devotion to Naomi," he said when she completed. *I shall not say a word about the weariness plaguing her eyes.* "Now, I will read to you. Perhaps a novel?"

"Not *David Copperfield,*" she whispered, covering her mouth to stifle a yawn. "The boys will be jealous. More of the Bible sounds fine, perhaps the Psalms. They are so soothing at the end of a long day."

"Excellent choice. I'll start with Psalm 119." Gabe thumbed through the pages, noting she grew more tired as time progressed. " 'Blessed are the undefiled in the way, who walk in the law of the Lord. Blessed are they that keep his testimonies, and that seek him with the whole heart. . . .' "

By the time, Gabe reached verse sixty, Lena had drifted asleep, her head resting on his left shoulder, her body completely relaxed. Being careful not to disturb her, he wrapped his arm around her frail shoulders. She snuggled closer, bringing a contented smile to his lips. He'd won in more than one way this night. Although he needed to quietly slip out to the barn, right now he wanted to close his eyes and bask in the joy of having her next to his heart.

He delighted in her face flushed with the firelight and her lips turned up slightly as if she enjoyed some wonderful dream. Tendrils of black had escaped from the hair carefully pinned at the back of her head to frame her oval face, and the thought of seeing those long silky tresses drape down over her shoulders filled him with pleasure. Such a sweet, altruistic soul. He felt dizzy with the moment, painfully aware of her nearness. Surely his sensibilities existed in an ethereal realm.

Daring to lean his head against hers, Gabe fought the urge to kiss her forehead. For the first time in his life he felt protective. *Oh, Father, is it so wrong of me to pray this angel of a woman might someday love me? I've vowed not to care that deeply, but she is breaking my will—or is it You acting on my behalf?*

How much longer he sat with Lena snuggled against him, Gabe did not know, only that this timeless moment must certainly be a glimpse of heaven.

Slowly he began to nod. As much as Gabe resisted allowing the closeness between him and Lena to fade, he must put her to bed. With more ease than he anticipated, he gathered her lithe body in his arms and slowly rose to his feet.

Lena neither stirred nor did her breathing alter. *I thought you slept like a feline.* As she lay against his chest, she sighed. Gabe wanted to believe she felt content because of him. Glancing down, he saw her face looked as smooth as a young girl's. She must have been a beautiful child.

He couldn't help but pull her closer, cradling her like he'd seen mothers carry their babies. He prayed she wouldn't waken, not because of his vow to sleep in the dugout, but because he wanted to relish in the softness of this sweet woman for as long as possible.

Gabe moved slowly into the bedroom. He clutched his wife with one arm and pulled back the quilts with the other. Gingerly he laid her on the straw mattress. The thought of removing her shoes crossed his mind, but he feared waking her. Instead, he covered her completely, tucking the blankets around her chin. No point in Lena Hunters falling prey to an illness.

Gabe studied her face. Even in the midst of darkness, he could see the peacefulness on her delicate features. It took all of his might to turn and leave, knowing the bitter cold of the barn awaited him.

"James," Lena murmured in her sleep.

Gabe shot a glance over his shoulder.

"James," she repeated barely above a whisper. "I miss you so much when you're gone."

ten

Gabe felt as though the bitter temperatures outside had taken roost in his soul. His reaction to Lena's honest emotions vexed him. How mindless of him to consider she might one day grow to care. He, Gabriel Hunters, the illegitimate son of a woman who once owned Philadelphia's largest brothel, would never compare to a decent man like Lena's deceased husband. How foolish for him to attempt such an inconceivable feat. He should have remained in Philadelphia, living in solitude and managing the monetary accounts of others. There his books were his friends, and they neither demanded of him nor ridiculed him.

Defeated before he even stepped foot on Nebraska soil, Gabe determined it best to return to the life he'd left behind. He could shelter himself from the cold, from people, and from the elements, and live out his days in peace.

Is that really what you want?

Shivering, Gabe ignored the inner voice.

Do you remember how My people grumbled after I delivered them out of Egypt from Pharaoh's cruelty? Were they not afraid and ready to return to slavery when they couldn't see My plan? Do you want freedom or a life enslaved in bitterness and loneliness?

Gabe's deliberations only took a moment: Caleb, Simon, and yes, Lena, promised more liberty than a ledger with worrisome numbers. Straightening, he turned his gaze into the fire. He could make an impact on these people's lives and learn how to farm. He could contribute useful information and encourage them in their spiritual walk with the Lord. Allowing the resentment from the past to take over his resolve meant the evil forces in this world had won. God hadn't promised him this family's love; He'd simply instructed Gabe to follow Him to Nebraska.

Turnip tilted his shaggy head as if the dog understood Gabe's silent turmoil. His tail thumped against the clay floor, offering no advice, only the gift of loyalty.

"Come along with me," Gabe whispered. "You and I have more in common than what others may cogitate." Slipping into his coat, he silently grimaced at the thought of one more night on a straw mattress. But with renewed confidence, he rolled up the three quilts for the trek to the barn.

Silently he made his way to the door with Turnip right behind him. The latch lifted with a faint click.

"And where do you think you're going?" Lena quietly demanded.

Gabe's gaze flew in her direction and he stiffened. *Caught.* "To the barn to sleep," he replied firmly.

In the shadows, his dear wife lifted a shotgun—the one that normally hung over the door. "I said that I did not intend to bury another husband. I know how to use this."

Gabe buried his face into the quilts to keep from laughing aloud and waking the boys or angering his wife. His earlier worries and fears, especially about James, contrasted with her resolve to keep him from the barn now seemed incredibly funny. He knew Lena's gun wasn't loaded. "Well, Mrs. Hunters, if I mean that much to you, then I shall surely sleep by the fire with Turnip at my feet."

≈

The following morning, three feet of fluffy white snow banked against the dugout and house and halted any plans to attend church. Lena gazed out at the dazzling display of winter's paintbrush. Smiling like a child with the first glimpse of a winter treat, she thought how much the boys would treasure playing outside this afternoon. She might even steal a moment with them.

Gone was the howling wind and threat of a death-chilling blizzard. In its wake, a quiet calm of white blanketed the land. The pure innocence in the aftermath of the storm reminded her of giving birth.

She watched Gabe trudge from the barn to the soddy. What had possessed her last night to pull the shotgun on him? This temper of hers had to be put to rest. My goodness, what if he had refused?

Once Gabe had resigned himself to sleeping by the fire, she'd crawled back into bed. Soon his laughter roared from the ceiling. In the next breath, she'd joined him, apologizing and holding her sides at the same time. If the boys woke, she never knew it, or maybe they simply enjoyed hearing the sound of merriment.

He is a delightful man, Lord. Why he puts up with my disposition is beyond me.

Leaning her forehead on the frosty glass window, she reflected a moment on the differences between James and Gabe. She hoped her contemplations were not wrong and quickly scanned her memory of the Bible to see if God would be disappointed in her comparisons. No particular verse came to mind, so she allowed her musings to continue.

James had enjoyed teasing her, sometimes unmercifully. After last night's episode, she realized Gabe possessed a delightful sense of humor too.

James didn't take much to book learning. He claimed nothing equaled the education of living life and taking each day as it came. Gabe placed a high regard on books and the importance of learning. Lena thought both men were right, but if she allowed herself to be truthful, she wanted her sons to have the opportunity of seeking professions other than farming if they so desired.

James sometimes grew so preoccupied with the workings of the farm that he neglected her and the boys—not because he didn't care for them, but because his love took the form of providing his very best. Gabe put his new family right under God. She'd seen him stop his work to give Caleb, Simon, or herself his undivided attention.

James's deeply tanned skin and dark hair had turned the heads of many women. Gabe's light hair and pale complexion reminded her of an albino mare her father once owned. With that horse, one had to look a little closer to find the beauty—but oh, what a gentle spirit lived inside. Lena had asked for the mare, and her father had consented, stating she recognized the value of a kind heart.

She held her breath. Remembering the albino and her father's words jolted her senses. Was there much difference between the mare and Gabe? A tear trickled down her cheeks as she realized the beginnings of love nestled in her heart.

How strange she could see so much of Gabe in such a short time. James and Gabe were notably different—each with their own strengths and weaknesses—equally good men. Before last night, she'd believed she'd never love another like James. But this morning's reflections caused her to think otherwise.

Gabe had carried her to bed, covered her, clothes and all. Not many men were that honorable. She sighed deeply and whisked away the tears. Now she understood the wisdom in Gabe desiring them to feel affection for each other before they consummated their marriage.

The latch lifted, and Lena waited expectantly for him to enter. Her heart fluttered, and she didn't attempt to stop it.

"Ah, Lena," he greeted, stomping his feet before stepping inside. "The boys and I have been conversing about all of this snow, and we'd like to take a stroll. Would you care to join us?" A sparkle of something akin to mischievousness met her gaze.

"Splendid," she replied.

He turned to leave, then added, "Leave the shotgun inside unless you think there's a wild beast that might threaten us."

Her eyes widened, and she giggled. "Oh, I don't know, Gabe. A nice wolf's pelt sounds like just the right thing." She pulled on her boots, then grabbed her coat, mittens, and wool muffler while he waited.

"Naturally, you'd need ammunition to protect us." They shared a laugh. "I do plan to take the rifle," he added. "Beauty can be deceiving."

"Yes, sadly so," she replied, feeling utterly content.

"In what direction is the school?" he asked a few moments later, as the boys chased each other in the snow.

Lena pointed northwest and squinted at the sun's reflection on the snow. "About two miles from here. Do you want to see for yourself?"

He nodded slowly. "Indeed."

"I imagine the soddy is in bad shape, being left empty and all. It needed repairs before we lost the teacher."

"Any prospects?"

She shook her head. "I don't think so. Haven't heard anyway."

They trudged along, stepping in and out of drifts. Gabe walked beside her, helping her through the deep piles of snow.

"It's unfortunate no one desires the teaching position," he said.

"Oh, the Shafer girl would love to fulfill it until a suitable person is found, but Dagget refuses. Says he needs her at home. Truth is, he's right."

"Is she capable?"

"I believe so. Amanda has a quick mind and certainly knows how to handle children."

"Hmm," Gabe replied, lifting the rifle to his shoulder. "This matter will take some thought. Perhaps I should pay a visit to Mr. Shafer in the morning when the boys deliver the milk."

"He'll run you off," Lena warned, her pulse quickening at the thought of how loathsome Dagget could be. "He's mean and selfish—almost as bad as me." She laughed, then sobered. "Really, Gabe, he is not a good father—works all of those children much too hard. I know our staple diet is cornbread and sorghum molasses, but he could butcher some meat for those children instead of selling his livestock to buy whiskey. Wouldn't take five minutes for you to see he doesn't care about them or their schooling."

Gabe lifted a brow. "But I don't give up easily, and if his daughter would make a fit teacher—"

"Good luck," Lena said. "He's as contrary as a sow with pigs—and just as dirty."

The crispness of the afternoon nipped at their breath and stung their cheeks, but Lena felt warm inside. For the first time in a long time, she felt safe. . .and content.

"Mama," Simon called.

She glanced in his direction and saw three white-tailed deer at the edge of a snow embankment. Like statues in the landscape, the deer suddenly leaped and bounded away—so graceful and effortless.

"You should have shot one, Gabe" Simon said. "Since Mama showed you how to use the rifle."

"Another day," Gabe replied. "Today is for pleasure, and I don't want to be killing an animal just for the sake of drawing blood. We have smoked venison at home."

Simon studied him curiously, then shrugged and took out after his brother.

"I'll take the boys hunting soon," Gabe said. "One at a time, though, so I can establish individual rapport. And if I haven't said it before, I appreciate your meticulous instructions on how to care for and use this rifle."

"You're welcome. I was amazed at your marksmanship after only a few tries." She smiled in his direction. "Of course, the Winchester is only as good as the one who fires it."

"Well, we shall see how skillful I am after a hunting expedition." Gabe chuckled. "Do we have elephants and lions out here? I sort of fancy myself as a hunter of ferocious beasts."

"Not likely, but we had a band of outlaws pass through here a few times."

He cringed, no doubt for her to see. "I'll take to bringing down a few geese or rabbits, if you can show me how to remove their outer coatings."

She shook her head. "We *skin* animals, and we *pluck* feathers from birds."

"I'll be sure to remember that."

Lena gasped and clutched Gabe's shoulder. "Oh, no. Dear God, no."

eleven

Gabe's attention flew to Caleb and Simon. They stood motion-less, paralyzed by a pack of wolves slowly encircling them. He heard the growls, saw the bared teeth.

Lord, no books ever prepared me for this. Help me. Help me, I beg of You. A quick assessment of Lena revealed a col-orless face.

Wordlessly, he took careful aim at a wolf closest to Simon. "Pray, Lena," he said, shielding any emotion. "God must deliver this bullet." Although tense, he focused on Lena's careful instructions from the past and all he'd read about the capabilities of the rifle.

"Don't move, boys," he called evenly. From what he'd read, running could prove disastrous. Holding his breath, he squeezed the trigger. A sharp crack splintered the air and star-tled the predators. One wolf howled and fell onto the snow, its blood staining the white ground.

"Steady," Gabe called to the boys.

Breathing a prayer of thanks and noting none of the ani-mals had inched closer, he sited another one, fired, and missed. He swallowed hard, neither looking to the right nor to the left. Again the wolves took a few steps back, and he squeezed a third in hopes they would disperse. "Get out of here," he shouted.

Help me, Father. Lena couldn't bear losing Caleb or Simon—and neither could I.

He dug his right-hand fingers into his palm, then released them before lining up a wolf straying too close to Caleb. This time, the bullet sunk into the wolf's neck. The cries of the injured animal pierced the air. In the next instant, Gabe fired at another one and missed. The rest of the pack moved beyond the circle, then one broke and raced in the opposite direction.

"Go on, get!" Lena cried. "Leave us alone!"

"Move back slowly," Gabe said to the boys. "Keep your eyes on those wolves, and do not panic." He fired another shot.

The animals watched Caleb and Simon's retreat, then turned and chased after the other lone wolf, disappearing into the scenery. Gabe studied the two he'd shot to make sure he'd killed them. One moved, and he sent a bullet into its skull.

"Thank You, Lord," Lena uttered.

Gabe heard her soft weeping and longed to comfort her, but she needed to embrace her sons and feel their young bodies safe and secure.

Simon and Caleb didn't show the emotion Gabe felt, but youth had a way of bouncing back after adversity. Once Lena had hugged them until they complained, Gabe dropped to one knee and wrapped his arms around them both. Tears filled his eyes, and he didn't strive to disguise them.

"I ain't, I mean I'm not calling you Gabe anymore," Simon said. "You're my pa, now."

Joy beyond Gabe's comprehension filled his very soul. *I never thought I'd be good enough. Thank You.*

"Some good shooting," Caleb said, staring at the dead wolves. "I don't think I'll ever forget today for as long as I live."

Tears coursed down Lena's cheeks. Gabe caught her gaze and her whispered words of gratitude. "Praise God for you, Gabe Hunters, and I bless the day you made me your wife."

He stared speechless, a rarity for him. Finally, he choked back a lump in his throat. "I think we can visit the schoolhouse another time," he said with a sniff. "I'd like to skin those animals—if one of you can tell me how—for new hats and mittens for you boys. Let's tend to it and move toward home. I'm in the mood for a snowball fight." He hoisted the rifle onto his shoulder and tossed a smile in Lena's direction.

Simon grabbed his free hand. "You might not know a lot of things, Gabe. I mean, Pa. But you stopped them wolves from eating me, and the other things don't matter."

Gabe couldn't reply for the overwhelming emotion assaulting him. He'd gone countless years without shedding tears, but today he'd made up for lost time.

"Listen to me, boys, while it's this cold and those wolves are venturing close, you won't be delivering any milk without me along, and I don't want you wandering far from home," he said.

"Yes, Sir," Caleb said with a smile. "Do you suppose you might teach me how to shoot, Pa?"

ॐ

Gabe slept by the fireplace that night. Once Simon cried out with a bad dream, and Lena crawled into bed with him. Gabe surmised she needed her arms around the boy as badly as Simon needed the affections of his mother.

Unable to sleep, Gabe rose early to milk and feed the animals. He felt a new confidence about his role in the family— a position he'd desperately craved but certainly hadn't wanted at the expense of yesterday's ordeal.

Today, he'd approach Dagget Shafer. Hopefully the man wasn't as formidable as the wolves.

"I don't have a good feeling about this," Lena said, as Gabe lifted the pail of milk into the wagon. "Dagget has no respect for anyone, including himself."

"A friend might redirect him. Does he claim to be a Christian man?"

"Gabe, he refused to attend his wife's funeral because it took him away from his farm." A torch flared in her eyes. "He treats those children horribly."

And he wanted you to marry him? "I'm pleased you

decided to accept my proposal instead of his, even if you had to run him off with a pitchfork." He chuckled, knowing the teasing would ease her trepidation.

She lifted a brow. "And how did you know about that?"

Gabe leaned over the side of the wagon and smiled into the face of this woman, this woman who had touched his heart like no one had before. "I'm having difficulty remembering. Perhaps it was the unsigned notice I received in Philadelphia warning me about your temper, or possibly the animals during those nights I slept in the barn—"

"Or Caleb and Simon," she interrupted. Covering her mouth, she shook her head, no doubt attempting to stifle her glee.

"But I have the distinction of you persuading me to your manner of thinking with a shotgun," he whispered.

She sighed and tilted her head. "Will you ever forget what I did?"

Gabe climbed up on the wagon seat and laughed heartily. "I rather doubt it. It's my ammunition." Calling for the boys to board, he picked up the reins and urged the horses on. "We'll return shortly, Lena, most likely a little better than an hour since I have business with Mr. Shafer."

"Do you have the rifle?" she asked as they pulled away.

"Yes, Ma'am. Danger won't find me unaware." At least he hoped not.

Gabe drove the team, a task he'd come to enjoy, while Simon chatted on about everything. Caleb, on the other hand, merely watched the landscape.

"You're quiet this morning," Gabe said. "Is a matter perplexing you?"

"I'm praying," the boy replied, picking at a worn spot on his trousers.

"Anything particular?"

He shrugged. "I don't want you to die like my pa. You didn't fit in so good in the beginning, but you do now."

Gabe realized the boy spoke from his heart. "A man doesn't choose what day God calls him home, but I have no intentions of doing anything foolish to quicken the process."

"I know that, but asking God to watch over you seems fitting to me."

"And I thank you. Life's been difficult since your father died."

"Yes, Sir." Caleb stared at the snow before them.

"Taking on the role as head of a household can be taxing."

"Yes, Sir."

Do I dare force his feelings out, Lord? Poor Caleb looks so miserable. "I'm sensing you didn't weep at the funeral."

A muscle twitched in Caleb's cheek, and his lips quivered.

Gabe continued. "My assumption is you knew your mother needed you, and so you pushed your grief aside."

Long moments passed with Simon's incessant talking to absolutely no one. A solitary tear slipped from Caleb's eye.

"Would you like to grieve the loss of your father now?" Gabe whispered.

Caleb nodded, his face so filled with sorrow that he threatened to burst. Gabe pulled the reins in on the horses and brought them to a stop.

"What's the matter?" Simon asked.

"Hush, Simon," Gabe chided gently. He turned to the older boy and enveloped him in his arms.

Caleb's tears began quietly, then proceeded to heavy sobs as his body heaved with the agony wrenching at his heart. *What do I say?* When God did not give him any words, Gabe remained silent.

For several minutes he held the boy, allowing him to spill out every stifled tear he'd ever swallowed. Gabe knew the healing power of physical grief; he'd been privy to it a precious few times when only God could comfort him. When Caleb withdrew from the shelter of Gabe's chest, he seemed humiliated.

"Don't ever regret showing emotion," Gabe said. "A real man attempts to experience all the happiness and sorrow the world contains. Only then can God use him in His perfect plan."

The boy offered a grim smile. "After today, He'll be using me for something big."

Meeting his smile, Gabe gathered up the reins and urged the horses on. *Is this what a father does? Lord, I'm exhausted from yesterday and today. . .but my spirit is exhilarated.*

The Shafer property bordered Lena's about forty minutes away, but instead of a sod-bricked soddy, the family's dwelling was a dugout—at least that's what it appeared to be. Many folks used this type of home, and Gabe understood the majority of homesteaders didn't have time to construct a soddy when they first arrived. Preparing the fields for crops took priority, and dugouts were quickly constructed for shelter.

The Shafer home and the two dugouts used for barns fell short of being called in shambles. All looked as if the roofs would cave in at any moment. A pig had climbed the snow-packed hill forming the home's roof. Gabe envisioned it falling through in the middle of a meal. Didn't sound like a good dinner guest to him. More pigs rooted up next to the house, leaving their droppings outside the door—a sharp contrast to the white landscape. Gabe had no tolerance for the lack of repairs, filth, or the ill-clad youngsters who met them.

"Mornin', Simon. Mornin', Caleb," a thin, pale boy said. His feet were bound with rags, and he didn't wear a coat.

"Mornin', Matthew," the boys chorused. One scratched his head, and the other spit, reminding Gabe of old men ready to sputter about the weather and their rheumatism.

"This is our new pa." Simon lifted the bucket of milk from the wagon.

Gabe climbed down and offered Matthew his hand. "Pleased to make your acquaintance. My name's Gabe Hunters."

Matthew didn't appear to know how to respond. He lightly grasped Gabe's hand and muttered something inaudible.

"Is your father available to speak with me?" Gabe asked, once again taking in the boy's scant clothing. "I'd like to introduce myself."

"He's with the pigs." Matthew pointed to a dugout nearby.

"Thank you." *I can follow the smell—even in the cold.* Gabe rounded the dugout. He heard a list of curses much like he used to hear from his mother's customers. Already he didn't care for Dagget Shafer.

"I told you to take care of this sow before breakfast, and it still ain't done," Dagget shouted. "Guess you need a beatin' to learn how to mind."

Echoes of yesterday assaulted Gabe, causing him to tremble with rage. "Mr. Shafer," he called out, forcing himself to sound congenial.

Another string of curses was followed by an "I don't have time to see callers." Dagget shuffled toward him, smelling like the animals he tended. "And who are you?"

Once again Gabe stuck out his hand. "Gabe Hunters. I'm your neighbor. Lena Walker's husband."

The man narrowed his brows and ignored Gabe's gesture of friendship. "Lena, ya say? She must have been looking for money, 'cause you don't look like a farmer to me."

And you don't possess any qualities resembling a decent human being. "I'm learning. I just thought it was about time I introduced myself."

"Why?"

"To be friendly, neighborly."

By this time, a little girl about three years old emerged from the shadows. She appeared clean from what he could tell, but her thin sweater and even thinner dress caused the child to shiver. In the shadows, a dark discoloration on her cheek indicated a bruise. Gabe didn't want to think how she might have been injured. The vile image of this man inflicting the blow brought back a myriad of his own beatings.

Bending, Gabe stared into the little girl's face. "Good morning," he said softly. She looked fearful and stepped back. "I'm Gabe Hunters."

The child recoiled as though he intended to harm her. She raced from the dugout, her sobs echoing behind her. Dagget broke into raucous laughter, further irritating Gabe.

"I'm sorry if I frightened your daughter," he said, still confused with what he'd witnessed.

"Aw, she thinks yer taking her to the Indians," Dagget said, between offensive guffaws.

"Why would she believe such a thing?"

Dagget wiped his face with a dirty coat sleeve. "I told her she'd best be ready 'cause I'd sold her to a man who'd trade her for blankets from the Indians."

He doesn't deserve any of these children. "What right do you have to tell a child such a terrible story?"

"It ain't no story. I'd do it in a minute. She ain't worth nothing, and it's none of your business no how."

Gabe stared into the haggard face. He seldom grew angry, but causing terror in a child incited a fury so great that it alarmed him. "You're right. Your daughter is not my concern, but I'm wondering why you don't pick on someone who can meet you as an equal."

Dagget narrowed his brows. "Like you? I'd make manure out of you in less than five minutes."

"Probably in less time than you might think, but I will say this. If you want to get rid of that child and any of your others, just bring them to our home. We'll take care of them in a proper manner."

Gabe whirled around and marched back to the wagon. What an insufferable beast and an even poorer excuse of a human being. No wonder Lena had refused his marriage proposal. He glanced at the dugout with an earnest desire to gather up every one of those children and take them home. Dagget would no doubt come after them once he needed work hands. Gabe looked to the heavens for answers. The thought of another child suffering through the same ordeal as he'd known infuriated him.

Lord, I know I utilize more of Your time than appropriate, but I'm pleading with You to look after these children. I've only met two of them and heard about four more, but You have them sealed in Your heart.

He'd met some wonderful hardworking people here in Nebraska—good citizens who loved the Lord and demonstrated their devotion to Him and each other in everything they said and did. Then there were a choice few who wouldn't know how to model the Lord if their lives depended on it. Gabe refused to dwell on Dagget another minute. He and Riley O'Connor were a matched pair.

Caleb and Simon stood near the wagon, still talking to Matthew. "Let's go, boys," Gabe said. "We have plenty of matters to tend to at home."

"Don't you be coming around here no more," Dagget shouted with a string of curses. "Them boys can bring the milk without the likes of you sticking your nose into my business."

Gabe took a deep breath and faced Dagget. "My sons will no longer be delivering milk. I will bring it each day but Sunday. If you want the milk for your family, then you'll deal with me."

He joined Caleb on the wagon seat, while Simon climbed onto the back. He released a labored breath and turned the horses toward home.

"I've never seen you mad," Simon commented a few moments later.

"I've never been so infuriated," Gabe replied. "Dagget Shafer places no value on his gift of children or the importance of the example he gives to them."

"I heard what you said to him back there," Caleb said. "I thought he was going to tear into you."

Gabe smiled grimly. "One punch would have flattened me, but I didn't care."

"I'd have helped you," the older boy said firmly. "We'd have done fine together."

Gabe wrapped his arm around Caleb's shoulders. The bond he and Caleb had formed felt good. *A father's love for his children.* "Your mother would have disciplined us severely for fighting, I'm sure."

"Naw," Simon piped up. "She doesn't like the way Mr. Shafer treats his children either. We don't tell her the things he says to us in the mornings."

A new surge of anger bolted through Gabe's veins. "Well, he won't have the opportunity anymore, now will he?"

twelve

"You're right, Gabe. It's snowing too hard to attend church tonight," Lena said with a disappointed sigh. Already at midday, she could barely see through the window for the driving snow. "I'd looked forward to driving into Archerville for the Christmas Eve services."

"We can conduct our own," Gabe replied with a reassuring smile. "It won't be the same for you, because I know how you enjoy visiting with the other members, hearing the sermon, and singing, but we'll honor the Lord's birth just the same."

"Oh, I know you're right, and you've looked forward to tonight too," she said. "I've noticed how you enjoy the minister's company." She tilted her head. "Seems like Christmas Eve should be spent with others, but we'll make do just fine."

"Of course we will. I'd like to involve the boys in our own little service, and I do have something for each of you."

"You do?" *When did he purchase gifts?* The occasions they'd ridden into Archerville for supplies, she'd been with him the entire time.

He offered a wry grin. "I purchased gifts in Philadelphia before boarding the train there."

"Mine are very small," she said, "and not fancy."

Gabe reached for her hand—an infrequent action for him. "You, Caleb, and Simon are my Christmas treasures. With you, I am the wealthiest man alive."

His words moved her to tears, for she knew without a doubt he meant every word. Although no mention of love had crossed their lips, she felt it growing as each day passed.

"Gabe, I have never met a man with such a giving spirit. I

feel as though you know our needs before we speak them."

His gaze met hers, sealing those words she wanted to say but couldn't—not until he spoke them first. "Next to God, my family is my life."

Oh, my dear Gabe. I never dreamed I could learn to love you, but you have made it easy.

That night after a hearty supper of ham, turnips, white-flour biscuits—which were a rare treat—and a pie made from dried pumpkins, they gathered around the fireplace to hear the Christmas story. Pushing back the rocker, all four sat on the rag rug. Caleb and Simon read from Luke, and Lena led in singing Christmas carols. Outside the wind whistled as it often did during snowstorms, but somehow it didn't sound threatening as the story of Jesus' birth unfolded before them.

"I have an idea," Gabe said, "one I think you'll enjoy. Caleb, I want you to pretend you are a shepherd boy. You've heard the angel's proclamation of Jesus' birth and are hurrying with the other shepherds to see the baby. Unfortunately, you must assist an aging shepherd who has difficulty walking. All the others leave you behind."

Caleb stared into the fire for a moment. He nibbled on his lip, then turned to Gabe. "Knowing me, I'd feel sad the other shepherds would see the baby Jesus before me."

"Only sad?" Gabe asked.

"Well, probably a little angry." Caleb glanced at his younger brother. "Sometimes when I have to wait for Simon to tag along with me, I get mad. He can't help being slow, like the old shepherd. Maybe I could talk to the old man so the walk would go faster."

"Very good." Gabe patted Caleb on the shoulder. "How do you think the old shepherd felt when the younger one had to help him walk to Bethlehem?"

Caleb brought his finger to his lip, seemingly concentrating on Gabe's question. "He might remember when he was young and didn't have to lag behind. I think he'd feel badly for the shepherd boy too."

"What would the two discuss along the way?"

"The angel's message?" Caleb asked without hesitation.

"Probably so," Gabe said.

Caleb took a deep breath. "And maybe how they all had been frightened when the angels appeared in the sky."

Lena listened in awe at the way Gabe taught the boys without them ever realizing it. *Caleb's always so serious. I wish he'd learn how to enjoy life before he's an old man.*

"And you, Simon?" Gabe continued. "What if you were the young shepherd boy?"

"Since the angels came at night, I might be a little afraid of wild animals."

"Much like the day with the wolves?" Gabe asked.

Simon's face grew serious. Nightmares had plagued his little mind since the incident. Many nights his cries awakened them all. "Yes, Sir."

"Don't you think if God cared enough for the world to send His Son as a baby that He might be watching out for all frightened boys?"

Simon gave Gabe his attention. "I think so. Do you think God cares about my bad dreams?"

Gabe ruffled Simon's hair. "I'm sure He does." He looked at each member of his family. Love clearly glowed from his gaze. "We all need to pray for Simon's nightmares until God stops them."

"I will," Caleb responded. "Those wolves were scary."

"Bless you, Son. We all need to pray for each other, in good times and bad." The room grew quiet, then Gabe spoke again, his tone lighter. "And now I have a gift for you."

The boys' eyes widened.

Gabe rose from the floor and walked to his trunk where he stored his books. The fire crackled, and Turnip rose on his haunches, his ears erect. "Easy, Boy. It's just the wind searching for a hole to get inside." Gabe retrieved a leather pouch and brought it back to the fire.

"You really did purchase these before you left Philadelphia?" Lena asked. "Why, you didn't even know us."

Gabe smiled, warming her heart. "I believed the future held something wonderful. . .and it did." He pulled out a small brown paper parcel. "This is for you, Simon."

The young boy grinned at his mother, then eagerly took the package. Inside, two carved wooden horses with soldiers mounted atop poised ready for a little boy to play with them.

"Thank you," he breathed, turning the toys over and over in his palm. A broad smile spread from ear to ear.

"And you, Caleb," Gabe said, handing him another parcel.

Lena watched her elder son slowly untie the string wrapped around his gift.

"A compass," Caleb whispered, moistening his lips. He peered up at Gabe with an appreciative gaze. "I will take good care of it always. I promise."

Gabe nodded. "I know you will. I know both of you take excellent care of your possessions." He turned to Lena. "And now for you." He strode over to the chest and pulled out a much larger package and handed it to her.

Oh, my. Has Gabe spent his money on something extravagant for me? It's large too. He gingerly placed the gift in her lap. "Open it, please," he said.

Lena swallowed a lump in her throat and slowly unwrapped the package, savoring the thought of Gabe's generous spirit more so than what was inside the package. She gasped, and her fingers shook as she lifted a cream-colored woolen shawl for all to see. "It's beautiful," she uttered, staring into his face. Never had he looked so handsome, so beloved as tonight. Every day his unselfish devotion amazed her, and every day her love for him grew. "Thank you so much. I've never had a shawl so grand."

"You're welcome." He smiled. "There's more for you." Gabe took the shawl and placed it around her shoulders.

Lena turned her attention to the remaining items in the package. Neatly folded yard goods in colors of light green and a deeper green plaid felt crisp to the touch. "How perfect," she whispered, examining the fabric and relishing its newness.

"I believe there's an ample amount of calico for a dress and jacket," he said.

"Oh, yes." She blinked back the tears. What was it about this man that drove her to weep for joy?

Gabe rubbed his hands together. "On our next visit to Archerville, I'd like to purchase the necessary items to make all of you new coats. And I believe new shoes and mufflers are also in order."

This time Lena did cry. She hadn't known where the money would come from to purchase the needed clothing for the boys. They grew so fast, and Caleb tended to wear out his clothes before Simon had an opportunity to wear them. "Oh, Gabe, you spent too much. Thank you, thank you ever so."

He lightly brushed his fingers over her hand. "I have a little put aside for our needs."

If I could only give to him what he's given to me and our sons. He loved her and the boys, of this she felt certain.

Lena hurried to the bedroom to fetch her own small packages. She'd saved for Christmas since last summer. For Caleb and Simon, she had bought peppermint sticks and had sewn them warm shirts. The ones they wore for everyday use were thin and had been patched many times. The boys thanked her and dutifully placed a kiss on her cheek.

She handed Gabe his package, believing he'd like it, but nervous nevertheless. Slowly he unwrapped the gift, and at first she feared he was displeased.

"Not a day passes I don't wish for a journal," he said, running his fingers over the leather cover. Still staring at it, he continued, "Humorous and serious bits of conversation, happenings I refuse to forget, something new I've learned, lessons our Lord has taught me. . ." He glanced up at her. "Memories are what keep us alive. Thank you, Lena. I'll treasure this always."

Her heart leaped to tell him those precious words, but she couldn't—not yet.

❧

"Stop it, Caleb!" Simon shouted as his face got thoroughly wiped with snow, courtesy of his older brother.

"What's the matter with a little snow?" Caleb asked, holding Simon down with one hand and reaching for another handful with the other.

"You know what I'm talking about." Simon sputtered and tried to punch him, but Caleb was faster and simply laughed. He coated Simon's face with the cold snow.

"Tell me," Caleb taunted.

"Pa," Simon hollered. "Caleb keeps hitting me in the face with snow that the cow did her business in."

Gabe groaned. *What would those two do next?* "Caleb, leave your little brother alone."

"Do you want to hear what he did to me this morning?" Caleb protested.

Not really, but I guess I will.

"He locked me in the outhouse for nearly an hour."

Gabe looked away to muffle his guffaw.

"You called me a runt," Simon retorted. "And took my quilt last night and wouldn't give it back."

"Boys, I have the perfect solution to this," Gabe said, wishing the boys could get along for one whole day without picking on each other. "Your mother is taking advantage of this cold weather by mending and such. The last I checked, she was preparing to darn socks—something each of you need to learn."

Simon stared at him incredulously. "That's woman's work!"

I feel a lesson coming on. "I believe your mother worked like a man before we married."

"That's right," Caleb said with an exasperated breath. "But since you've been here, Ma doesn't have to do that anymore."

Gabe lifted a brow. "Then show your gratitude. Inside, boys."

"Yes, Sir."

"Yes, Sir."

Caleb and Simon plodded to the soddy. Gabe grinned and turned his attention back to rearranging the tools inside the barn. He wondered what they'd think of next.

ॐ

Had four months really passed since Gabe arrived in Nebraska? The days flew by, each one blending into the next. He loved every moment of it, not once ever considering the natural demands of his family and farm as a hardship.

As had been his habit since the first morning, Gabe woke at the hint of dawn. He'd grown accustomed to sleeping on the tamped earthen floor by the fire, long since comprehending he had the warmest spot in the soddy, but this morning an eerie shriek of wind woke him. The howls carried a sense of foreboding, different than other bouts with high winds that ushered in heavy snowfall. Gabe's concerns mounted for the livestock. They had a goodly stock of supplies and provisions, but he feared losing any of the animals to the cold. When the temperatures had plummeted in the past, the dugout had provided sufficient protection to ensure the warmth of the horses, mule, and chickens. But the cattle in the fields could not huddle close to a warm fire.

After slipping his overalls overtop his trousers and pulling his suspenders up, Gabe quickly added chips to the fire. *Thankfully, we can keep the soddy warm.*

"You're up earlier than usual," Lena said quietly. "I'm afraid we're in for a bad storm." In the shadows her silhouette and soft voice comforted him. His love for her abounded in moments like these. The freshness of sleep on her lovely face tempted him to reveal his heart. Fear of her rejecting him always halted his confession. He believed she cared and often saw something akin to affection in those green eyes, but he could be mistaken.

"Winter winds are attacking us again," he said, making his way to the peg holding his outer garments. As he shrugged into his coat, he fretted over past snows. "Lena, how did you survive the winters alone? How did you deal with all of the work and responsibilities of this farm?"

"By God's grace," she answered. "When the wind tore around the soddy and snow banked against the door, or when in the heat of summer, tornadoes raged, I simply prayed." She walked across the room and took his muffler from his hands. Wrapping it around his neck, she smiled. "God's never failed me. Somehow I managed to make it through one perilous situation after another. Then He sent me you." Her last words were spoken barely above a whisper.

Gabe warmed to his toes. Was she conscious of what her sweetness did to him? The emotion bursting inside him sought to surface. He longed to take her into his arms and declare his love. *Oh, Lord, dare I?*

"Tonight, after Caleb and Simon are in bed, I'd like to discuss a matter with you." Gabe instantly regretted his choice of words. He sounded as though he wanted to propose a business transaction. "I mean, do you mind talking with me for awhile?"

"Is everything all right?" she asked, pulling her shawl around her shoulders.

"I believe so." He dipped his hands into each mitten. "It's not a topic you need to worry about, just a personal matter about which I wanted your opinion." He offered a smile and grasped the latch on the door. "Come along, Turnip. We have work to do. From the sound of the wind, I may be blown to Archerville."

She laughed lightly. "I'd come looking."

Would you, my love? "How far would you venture?"

"As far as Philadelphia, and if you weren't there, I'd look some more."

thirteen

Outside, the biting cold and wind whipped around Gabe's body with a fury he'd never experienced. He fought to stand and instead fell twice to his knees. The very thought of Lena and the boys existing in this ominous weather filled him with dread. Surely God had watched over them.

Once the animals were fed and cared for, he gathered up the quarter pail of milk and trekked back to the house before dawn. Only one of the cows had not gone dry, and the others had been turned out to pasture when they'd stopped producing milk. He caught a glimpse of the winding smoke from the fireplace, and he knew his family welcomed him inside. As always, Lena would have coffee ready.

Although the faint light of morning tore across the sky, he couldn't study the clouds for the curtain of snow assaulting him from every direction. He'd studied clouds in his books and, together with Lena's teachings, had learned to read nature's map. This morning spelled blizzard, and already all he could see of the cabin was the fire twinkling through the window. Suddenly the wisp of smoke from the chimney vanished.

The Shafers would miss their ration of milk today, but he dared not risk losing his way in the snow. He'd missed bringing them milk before, and they had fared well. Obviously, this was a day to advance the boys in their lessons.

"Turnip," he called. Normally the dog came bounding. "Turnip." Gabe released a heavy sigh. He pondered looking for the animal. However, once he ventured out again into the blinding snow and ferocious wind, he abandoned his purpose, setting his sights on the beacon in the cabin window.

Turnip is probably in the house, lying by the fire all snuggly warm. Deserter.

Each step took his breath and cut at his face. He contemplated resting the pail on the snow and pulling the muffler tighter around his face but feared spilling the contents. If the blizzard raged on, they might need the milk.

"Gabe!" Lena called.

He glanced toward the cabin.

"Gabe!"

"Yes, I'm making progress," he replied, the wind stinging his throat. "I see the firelight in the window."

"I'm waiting for you."

The dearest words this side of heaven. He'd stumble through ten blizzards for that endearing sound. "Don't linger in the cold," he called to her. "You'll be ill."

"Not until you get here."

Stubborn woman, and he loved her for it.

Once he reached the front door, she opened it wide. A gust of wind sent it slamming so hard on the inner wall of the cabin that he feared the house would crumble. She stood covered from head to toe with the new coat, mittens, and muffler he'd purchased in Archerville. She reminded him of an Egyptian mummy he'd seen in a book.

"I should have given you a rope," she said, shaking the snow from her coat.

"To tie about my waist and to the house?"

She nodded. "Don't leave again without it. You could wander around for hours and freeze to death."

He chuckled. "I know you've expressed concern over that condition before." He hung his outer garments on the peg beside hers. The aroma of coffee mixed with frying cornmeal flapjacks filled his nostrils.

"Ready for coffee?" she asked, as if reading his thoughts.

"Absolutely." He walked to the fireplace and glanced

around for the dog. "Isn't Turnip inside?"

She whirled around and stared at him. "No. He left with you."

Where is the dog? He shivered, both from the bitter cold and the prospect of Turnip caught in its grip. "I need to find him."

"Later, Gabe. You need to get out of those wet clothes." She hesitated. "You've lost so much weight I believe you could wear James's clothing. Let's take a look. We can deal with the dog after breakfast."

He followed her into the bedroom, feeling slightly uncomfortable with the unmade bed and the fresh scent of her lingering in every corner. If he were to wake up tomorrow and find himself blind, he'd live out his days with her face in his mind.

Lena pulled a trunk from beneath the rope bed and sorted through it. Gabe stood back, uncertain if he should invade her personal treasures.

"Here's a shirt and overalls," she said, handing him the carefully folded clothing. "I'm sure they will fit."

"Will this plague you or the boys? Seeing me in his attire?"

She shook her head. "He'd be pleased they'd come to good use, and so am I." She stepped from the small room and pulled a curtain separating the bedroom from the main room. "Do you mind if I let the boys sleep?"

"Let them," he replied, examining the shirt and overalls. He felt oddly disconcerted by the knowledge that they'd belonged to Lena's deceased husband. "Not much for them to do today with the blizzard." *And I need to find Turnip.*

Gabe donned the clothes and caught sight of himself in Lena's dresser mirror. *I look so different—not at all like the Gabriel Hunters who left Philadelphia. What happened to my portly body?*

In the midst of his second cup of coffee and a third flapjack smothered in molasses, he looked up to see Caleb making his way through the blanket separating the boys' room from the fireplace and cookstove.

"Mornin'," he greeted through sleepy eyes. "Sounds like we have a blizzard. Strange, we haven't had one all winter."

"We do, Son," Gabe replied. "My first Nebraska blizzard, and it's everything this family has warned. We'll all stick close to the fire today; maybe do a little extra reading."

Caleb grinned. "Sounds good to me." Glancing about, he gave his mother a puzzled look. "Where's Simon and Turnip?"

Lena's face turned a ghastly shade of pale. She swallowed hard and called out. "Simon, are you using the chamber pot?"

No answer.

"I woke up, and he wasn't there," Caleb said softly. "He wouldn't have wandered outside, would he?"

Gabe rose and made his way to the boys' room. His coat. He prayed Simon's coat hung on the peg beside his pallet.

"Simon?" Lena called, her voice anxious. . .and scared.

"He's not here." Gabe hurried to the front door. He couldn't face Lena. First he'd lost Turnip, and now Simon had disappeared. "I'll find him," he said as he grabbed his winter garments. By the time he'd pulled on his mittens and wrapped the muffler around his face to bar the frigid cold, Lena had a rope.

"Tie one end around your waist and the other around one of the porch posts," she said shakily.

He couldn't avoid eye contact any longer. "I'll not disappoint you or Simon." Not waiting for her reply, he stepped out into the blizzard, praying harder than when he'd faced the wolves. At least then he could see his son and the face of danger. He felt his way to the right post anchoring the porch.

"Simon, where are you?" he called, but the wind sucked away his breath, and the words died in his throat. Securing the rope, he plodded toward the barn.

I've always had a keen sense of direction, but not even a compass could assist me now. Oh Lord, be my feet and lead me to Simon.

"Simon, Turnip," he tried calling again. The roar of the wind met his ears.

After what he believed was several minutes, he bumped into the well. He'd walked in the opposite direction! Making his way around it until he could grab the well handle, Gabe closed his eyes and turned in the direction of what he believed was the barn. Every second became a prayer. On he went, his feet feeling as though they were laden with weights. The way seemed endless, and ofttimes he fell.

"Pa." He strained to hear again. "Pa, I'm scared and cold."

Praise God. Simon must be in the barn. Guide me, Lord.

Gabe tried to speed his trek, but the elements slammed into him as though an invisible wall had been erected. "I'm coming, Simon. Have faith."

With his chest aching and each step an effort, Gabe at last touched the side of the dugout where he believed Simon awaited inside. "Simon, I'm by the barn wall."

Nothing. Not even the hint of sound indicating the boy rested safely inside.

Gabe repeated his words. *Keep him in Your arms. I beg of You.* Rounding the barn, he found the opening. A few moments later, he stepped inside and scanned the small area. A pair of arms seized him about the waist. Gabe wrapped his arms around Simon, wanting to shelter him forever from the cold and wind.

"You came," Simon said between sobs. "I thought I'd die here with Turnip and the animals."

Turnip's tale thumped against Gabe's leg. Never had the dog looked so good. "I heard you calling for me," Gabe said, carefully inspecting him from head to toe. Luckily, the boy had dressed warmly before leaving the cabin.

Simon shook his head. "I didn't call for you. I just waited and talked to God about being scared."

Thank You, Lord, for sending Your angels to minister to me and keep Simon safe. Joy raced through Gabe's veins, while he hugged the boy closer.

"You're the best pa ever," the boy said, clinging to Gabe's snow-covered body.

"We must give the credit to our Lord," Gabe replied, tucking Simon's muffler securely around his neck and face. "Oh, Simon, what made you decide to come looking for Turnip?"

"I didn't. I heard you get up early and wanted to help with the chores, but with the blizzard, I couldn't find the barn. Turnip guided me here, but you were already gone."

The dog nuzzled Gabe's leg, and he patted him. No doubt, God had used stranger-looking angels than a mangy dog.

"We need to head back. Your mother and brother are very worried. First, let's check on the animals and pray."

And they did, thanking God for taking care of Simon and sending His angels to help Gabe.

"Ready?" Gabe asked, dreading the walk ahead.

Simon nodded. "Don't let go of my hand, please."

"I'll do better than that. I'll carry you." Although Gabe wondered how he'd make it back with the extra load, he knew God hadn't brought him this far to desert him now. He'd follow the rope. Gathering up Simon, he whispered, "Keep your head down against the wind, and pray."

"Yes, Pa. I love you."

&

Lena could wait no longer. Gabe had been gone an hour, with every minute taking a toll on her heart. She must do something.

"Caleb, I'm going out there. I'll follow the rope, so don't worry." Pulling on her heavy clothes, she ignored her son's protests.

"Then, I'm going with you," he said stubbornly, reaching for his coat.

"I won't lose two sons in this blizzard."

"And I won't lose my ma, pa, and brother either."

Bravery doesn't need to be so dangerous. "I want you to stay here, please."

Caleb stood before her dressed for the weather. "I'm going with you." He lifted the latch. "We'll both follow the rope."

Lena made her way to the post, but the rope was gone. She searched the other side of the porch. Nothing. She kneeled on her hands and knees, frantically searching for the loose end. She felt certain Gabe had secured his end to the right side. Caleb joined her. The wind stole her breath, but she refused to give up. The snow could have covered the rope in a matter of moments, but without it, Gabe would never find his way to the cabin. She prayed and wept—for Simon, Gabe, and the love she possessed for both of them.

Caleb tugged at her coat. She ignored him. He tugged harder and began to drag her back. "I found it," he shouted.

Lena wrapped her fingers around the frayed ends and clung to it as though she held the hand of God. She and Caleb managed to crawl back onto the porch and to the door. Securing the rope around the porch post had proved useless. She'd not let it go until she saw her family. *Help them, Father. Bring them back to me.*

"I'll stay out here and hold it," Caleb shouted above the wind.

"No, I'm stronger. Go back inside."

"I'm nearly twelve, Ma, and I'm staying."

He sounded so much like James, so much like Gabe—so much like a man. She didn't argue.

Lena's whole body grew numb with the cold. Every so often she stomped her feet and forced her body to move. Caleb followed her example. *Where are they?*

Then the rope moved. Perhaps the wind had grasped it and toyed with her mind. She felt another pull and grabbed Caleb's arm.

"They're coming! I can feel it." She laughed and cried at the same time, simply believing Gabe had Simon. After all, he'd said he'd bring back her son—their son.

The minutes dragged on before she caught sight of Gabe trudging through the snow, carrying Simon with Turnip beside them. For a moment, she feared her eyes might deceive her, but then Caleb called out to Gabe, and he answered. Tears froze on her cheeks.

Once the wind and snow lay outside and she saw Simon and Gabe were safe, Lena threw her arms around Gabe's snow-laden body and sobbed on his chest.

"Simon's fine," Gabe soothed. "He was in the barn with Turnip staying warm with the animals."

"I was afraid I'd lost you both. Oh, you dear, sweet man, I love you so."

fourteen

She. . .she loves me? Surely I'm mistaken. She must mean Simon. Gabe pushed Lena's show of exuberance to the far corner of his heart. Later he'd contemplate those words when solitude embraced his mind and body.

A shiver rippled through Gabe's body, and he suddenly noticed that his teeth were chattering uncontrollably. Practical matters must be addressed first.

Gabe thought he'd be freezing till the day he crossed over the threshold from earth to heaven. . .and poor Simon. Even sitting by the fire and cocooned in a blanket, the boy still shivered.

A teasing thought passed through Gabe's mind. "When I was in Philadelphia, I read about this doctor who believes we all would be healthier if we took a bath every day rather than once a week."

Caleb and Simon's eyes widened in obvious disbelief.

"Might be a little cold to start that today, don't you think?" Gabe asked and caught an amused glance from Lena. "Although, if you want, I could bring in enough snow to melt for the tub."

"Not today," Simon replied. "I'd rather work on my lessons all day until it's dark."

Laughing, Lena kissed Simon's cheek. "Drink this," she said gently.

"What is it?" He stared at the cup of brown-colored liquid.

"Tea with honey. It will help you get warm on the inside."

Simon peered up at Gabe as though looking for his approval. "Yes, drink it. You'll be glad you did. I'm having plenty of coffee to warm me up. Our insides are cold, Son."

The boy nodded and reached through the blanket for the tea. Gabe smiled. Lena was right when she said Simon usually did the totally unexpected. He'd never offered to help with chores before. And to venture out on this horrendous day? No one in this household would ever doubt the presence of God. Gabe carefully recorded the story in his journal to read when the problems of life seemed overwhelming. After he'd told Lena about thinking he'd heard Simon's voice call out to him, she'd cried again.

Her endearing words when they entered the cabin still nestled deep in his heart. Had she really meant them, or was she simply filled with gratitude? Emotion often guided a woman's response to external stimuli, and he fully understood if she'd simply overreacted in her enthusiasm to find Simon safe. But he desperately wanted to believe otherwise.

She handed him another cup of coffee. "Are you doing all right?"

"Yes, thank you." *Her very presence intoxicated him.*

"Do you still want to talk to me about something tonight?" *Even more so.* "If you're not exhausted."

She smiled and laid her hand on his shoulder. "I have a topic of my own, if you're not too tired."

Simply listening to your voice fills me with joy. "We will have a good evening together." Speaking more softly, he added, "You are an excellent wife, Lena. As I said on our wedding day, I'm honored."

She blushed, and her reaction surprised him. Clearly flustered, she rose and wrung her hands. "Ah, Caleb, would you like to get the Noah's Ark from the chest under my bed? I think Simon would enjoy playing with it."

"And when you're finished, I'll read to you," Gabe added. "I have a new book I believe you will enjoy."

"It's not about snow, is it?" Simon asked, holding his cup with both hands. "Or wolves?"

Gabe chuckled. "No, Son. The book is called *Moby Dick* by Herman Melville. The story is about a whale and a sea captain."

Simon grinned before taking a sip of tea. "I can hardly wait."

"Me too," Caleb echoed from the other room. "A real adventure. Might I read a bit of it aloud?"

"Most assuredly." In times like these, Gabe forgot the boys' pranks and mischievous ways and dwelled on his intense love for them and all they represented.

The day passed quickly with quiet activity. While Gabe read, Lena sewed by the fire. When evening shadows stole across the sky, she prepared corn in one of the thirty different ways she knew to use it. The challenge had become a joke to them, especially when they all grew tired of cornbread, mush, flapjacks, and molasses.

Lena possessed a radiance about her that he didn't quite understand; perhaps her glow came from the fact Simon had not frozen to death. These past four months had seen both lads in perilous circumstances. Was this the way of raising children? He'd rather think not, but the logical side of him told him otherwise. No wonder parents' hair grew gray. He'd always attributed it to wisdom, but now he credited the color difference to the hardships of parenting. In reflecting on his past, Gabe knew without a doubt that he wouldn't trade one moment with his family.

God, You have blessed me beyond my most secret thoughts. All I can say is thank You.

Once the boys were in bed, Lena tended to her sewing while Gabe wrote in his journal, recording every moment of the day.

I thank the Lord for His deliverance today, he concluded. *Now, I cannot let the words of my heart stay imprisoned any longer. I will tell Lena this evening of my love for her. To hold it back any longer would be to deny my very own existence.*

He closed the book and set it aside. Now that the words were in print, he must brave forward.

"Would you like another cup of coffee?" Lena asked.

He studied her cherished face as he mustered the courage to begin. "No, thank you."

She drew her rocker closer to his chair. "Are you plenty warm?"

"Yes, I'm content." His heart began to pound more furiously than drummers in a parade. "You mentioned your desire to speak with me about a matter."

She nodded and stared into the fire. Her cheeks flushed, kindling his curiosity.

"You're not becoming ill, are you?" He leaned up on his chair to view her more closely. The thought of touching her forehead crossed his mind.

"Oh, no. I'm perfectly fine," she hastily replied.

Easing back, he folded his hands across his once ample stomach. "Go ahead, I'm listening."

She rose and paced back and forth in front of the fire. "Do you remember what I told you this morning when you returned with Simon?"

She's full of regret. I surmised as much. "Yes, I do remember." With great effort, he stared up into her face.

Slowly, she removed her apron and laid it across the rocker. Inhaling deeply, she sat in front of him on the rug. "I meant every word," she whispered.

Gabe thought his heart had stopped.

She moistened her lips. "I've known for weeks, but I didn't want you to think of me as brash." Lowering her head, she picked at a loose tuft on the rug.

Have I heard correctly? Is this a dream? But when he glanced at the top of her head, he dared not lose his nerve. Gently he lifted her chin and smiled into those green pools he'd grown to cherish.

"And I have loved you for weeks, but I was uncertain of your response."

She looked innocent, fragile, her lovely features silhouetted by the fire, her pursed lips equally inviting. Gabe bent and kissed his wife. It was a soft kiss, a tender kiss, but a luxury that invited more. . .and more.

"I do love you, Lena," he whispered. "You are my life and my joy. I never dreamed I'd be so blessed."

She drew back from him. With a sweet smile, she pulled the pins from her raven-colored hair and allowed the long tresses to cascade down her back. Taking his hand, she said, "I believe it's time we became man and wife."

ا

Lena woke and wiped the sleep from her eyes. Sometime during the night the winds had stopped. Gabe had risen in the wee hours of the morning and tried not to stir her, but she knew the instant he'd climbed out of bed. For two weeks now, they'd been true husband and wife, and she treasured their tender relationship.

"Go back to sleep," he'd whispered earlier. "The snowstorm is over, and I want to check on the cattle."

"I'll go with you," she said, unable to bear the thought of him leaving her side. She'd become unashamedly possessive.

He'd leaned over and kissed her. "No, my dear. I won't be long." For the first time in years, she felt loved and protected. Her eyes closed. How wonderful to love and be loved. Surely this would last for a hundred years.

Now, as morning graced the skies and the shades of rose and amber ushered in the dawn, Lena met the day with happiness and hope for the future. She had a husband who cherished and adored her—and considered her sons as his own. What more could she ever ask?

This morning he planned to ride over to the Shafers and make sure they had fared well during the storm. Most likely the snow held drifts in some places higher than the cabin. She and Gabe had already experienced the snow drifting to the top of their door, holding them captive within their home.

Lena sighed and listened to see if Caleb and Simon were up. She should go with Gabe. Dagget despised her husband, ridiculing him each morning when he brought milk. Gabe had asked him one day if he detested his presence so much, then why didn't he buy a cow. However today, the children wouldn't get any milk until the wagon could get through.

As she dressed, her thoughts drifted back to those first few weeks when Gabe had tried so hard to learn everything he could about the farm. He'd hammered his thumb, spilled a bucket of milk, spooked the horses while learning to drive the wagon, and nearly gotten sprayed by a skunk. The dear man did not give up, even when drenched by a downpour in the midst of patching the dugout roof. She'd admired his courage and stamina. Every day a new adventure brought them closer—even the unpleasant and frightening challenges. There had been a time—and not so long ago—when she'd believed no man could ever take James's place. How wrong she'd been. God had indeed brought her the best.

≥∙

God had indeed brought Gabe the best. He treasured his family and their relationship. Two weeks ago, he and Lena had confessed their love for each other, and now he actually felt like a married man. Never had he dreamed his life might contain such fulfillment. Oh, there were disagreements here and there, and Simon would always be unpredictable, but to have his heart's desire fulfilled. . .well, he simply couldn't put a price on what it all meant to him. When Lena looked at him with her impish smile, he melted faster than the snow in spring.

This morning, he had a job to do. Neither the cold nor the snow could stop him from braving the elements to reach the

Shafers. He worried about the Shafer children, especially when he noted the many times sour, old Dagget had been drinking by the time he arrived with milk. He'd seen the scurvy sores on the children's thin arms and faces, and Lena had sent dried fruit and vegetables to add more nutrition to their diet. Caleb and Simon had passed their old coats, mittens, mufflers, and hats on to them, but Gabe doubted if Dagget even noticed.

The Shafer children were mannerly, and Gabe had allowed Amanda to borrow a few books. She always thanked him, eager to report on what she'd read and often pointing out confusing words for his explanation. He appreciated her willingness to educate herself, especially in this part of the country where most women lived to bear children and work the farms. Amanda had done her best to school her brothers and sisters with a McGuffey Reader, but she didn't have any slates or chalk. Gabe found extra in his trunk so she could teach them to write and learn arithmetic.

Smoke curled above the dugout in the distance. He breathed a sigh of relief. He'd feared their home had caved in with the weight of the snow. An abundance of it had fallen in the last two weeks, so much he'd climbed onto the roof of his house and barn to clean them off.

The image of the little Shafer girl with her bruised face and obvious terror haunted him. Not once had he seen her since she ran from him, Dagget's repugnant laughter echoing through the barn.

Dismounting his horse, Gabe saw the door had more than three feet of snow banked against it. Not seeing a shovel, he used his gloved hands to scoop a path wide enough for the door to open. He knocked soundly. Amanda answered, her eyes red. A whimpering child could be heard in the background.

"Good morning, Mr. Hunters. I'm glad to see you are all right from the storm."

Something is wrong here. "I came by to see how you were fairing after the snowstorm. I apologize for not having milk, but the drifts are too high for the wagon. I believe the cow is about to go dry too."

Her round face, pale and rigid, looked distracted. "Thank you, but we are warm and have plenty of chips for the fire."

"And food?"

"We will manage. I appreciate you stopping by." She hesitated, then whispered, "I can't let you in, Mr. Hunters. Pa would thrash me for sure."

He smiled in hopes of easing her nervousness. "I understand, Amanda. Is—"

"Amanda, whata ya doing?" Dagget's slurred voice bellowed.

She glanced behind her. "It's Mr. Hunters."

"Shut the door!" A string of curses followed with how Dagget viewed his daughter and Gabe, certainly nothing complimentary.

"I'll not keep you," Gabe said to Amanda. "Let us know if we can be of assistance."

Amanda's eyes pooled as she slowly shut the door. Gabe offered another reassuring smile and ambled toward his horse.

"Wait," Amanda called from the doorway. "We do need help. Mary is awful sick—burning up with fever."

Gabe whirled around. "What have you given her?"

"I don't have anything but a little ginger tea, and I've applied a mustard plaster. Pa had me give her whiskey and a little molasses, said it would cut the cough and put her to sleep. Mr. Hunters, did I do the right thing? Ma always said spirits invited evil."

"Amanda, get in here now! I'll teach you to mind me."

Dagget had been drinking, that was obvious, but Gabe wasn't about to ride home and forget the little girl lying sick. He strode back to the door and entered the small dugout. It smelled rank from whiskey, vomit, and unkempt bodies.

The little girl stared up from a straw pallet with huge, cavernous eyes, the same child from the barn incident weeks before. She coughed, a deep ragged sound that rattled her chest. Her little body shook, and she barely had enough strength to cry. Nearby, Dagget sat sprawled in a chair with a bottle of liquor in one hand and the other clamped around Matthew's wrist. In the shadows, three boys ranging from about Simon's age to probably fifteen sat motionless.

Gabe clenched his fists and fought the rage tearing through him. He swallowed his anger, realizing a fight with Dagget would solve nothing. "A good father would put down that bottle and see what he could do about nursing this child."

Dagget lifted a brow. "She ain't none of yer business. So ya'd best be leaving before I find my shotgun."

"Not yet," Gabe said quietly, edging closer to view the child's pallor.

Dagget staggered to his feet and took a swallow from the bottle. Finding it empty, he threw it across the room. The pieces landed dangerously close to the boys huddled in a corner. "Git me my gun, Charles."

fifteen

The older boy emerged from a corner, a strapping young man, tall and muscular. He glanced at his little sister suffering through another gut-wrenching cough, then at Amanda. "No, Pa. I'm not getting you the gun."

Dagget swung his arm wildly. He released Matthew and stood to stagger toward Charles. "Boy, you'll know this beatin' for a long time."

Lord, why are there such animals in this world? "You'll not harm him," Gabe said, surprising himself with his firmness.

"It's all right, Mr. Hunters," Charles said. "He's too drunk to do anything but talk, and we've all had enough. Truth be known, I could take him on, but I don't like the idea of fighting my own pa."

"Why you—"

Gabe grabbed Dagget's arm and shoved him back down onto the chair—the first time he'd ever touched a man in fury. "Stay put, because I intend to make sure this child is properly tended to."

"If only the doc didn't live so far away," Charles said, bending to feel Mary's forehead, while Amanda wiped her face with a damp cloth.

"It would take four days or more to get him," Gabe replied, thinking Dagget was angry enough without Charles adding more rebellion by leaving. "She needs attention now, and that's a rough journey for a grown man."

"No disrespect meant, but it's time I acted like a man and took better care of my brothers and sisters. Pa never acted like this when Ma was alive, and he treats Mary like a pitiful

116

dog." Charles shook his head. "It's not her fault ma died giving birth to her, but Pa expects her to pay for it every day."

"Seems like she doesn't want to fight this sickness," Amanda added. "It's as though she's given up."

"I have to do something." Without another word, Charles reached for a thin coat on a peg beside the door. "I need to get help somewhere."

"Go to Lena. She has more tea and some herbs to nurse your little sister." Gabe began to pull off his own outer garments. "Here, take my coat. It's warmer. And my horse is already saddled."

Charles hesitated.

"Do take the coat and Mr. Hunters's horse," Amanda insisted. "You don't need to be ill too."

Reluctantly, Charles accepted the clothes. A handsome lad with light hair and strong features, he stole another glimpse at Mary. "Thank you, Mr. Hunters, and I apologize for not expressing my gratitude in the past for the milk."

"It's quite unnecessary," Gabe said. "Hurry along. The snow is deep, and it will take you a few hours to get there and back."

Nodding toward his father, Charles asked, "Do you want me to tie him up?"

Excellent idea. "No. I can handle Dagget just fine."

After he left, Gabe greeted the other children. They appeared a bit leery of their father, who only stared into the flames. He didn't bark any orders or curse. He simply sat.

Amanda made Mary as comfortable as possible, wrapping her in another blanket and moving her closer to the fire, while Gabe scooted Dagget's chair away from it.

Nearly three hours later, Lena and the boys arrived. Simon road on the horse, while the other three traveled on foot. Charles carried food, ginger for tea, and another potion of dried horseradish to brew for Mary. Lena and the boys carried dried elderberries, salt pork, a little milk, and a blanket.

"None of us wanted to wait at home when we might be of use here," Lena said. "The walk felt refreshing after being inside all day yesterday."

"I'm glad I didn't know you were trekking across the snow, but I'm glad you're here." Gabe helped her remove her coat and kissed the tip of her nose—so natural a gesture, so easy now that she'd revealed her heart and accepted his love.

Lena's presence eased the heaviness threatening to overwhelm him. To him, anger had always been a characteristic of the weak, and a trait he'd refused to succumb to. The sins accompanying loss of control were vile. *I've never felt so angry. I don't know whether to apologize to Dagget or try to make him comprehend what he's doing to his family.*

Caleb and Simon urged the younger boys to head outside. Gabe surmised the Shafer children didn't share the luxury of free time very often, although their lack of proper clothing tugged at his conscience.

"Check on the hogs," Dagget bellowed. "And feed my mules."

Gabe said nothing for fear he'd strike the man. Every muscle in his body tensed, ready to shake him until what few teeth he had fell out.

He definitely did not feel like the model of a godly man.

"Why?" Dagget asked of Gabe a few moments later. "You bring milk 'most everyday. You're ready to fight me over—" He pointed to Mary.

"Can't you say her name?" Gabe asked, the ire swelling inside of him again. *Lord, I'm being self-righteous here. Dagget is wrong, but it's not right for me to condemn him.*

"She killed her ma." Bitterness edged Dagget's words.

Gabe glanced at the child. If she died, God would lift her into His arms in heaven. If Dagget died, what would be his fate? "God took your wife home and left you a gift. In fact,

He left you with six treasures. Maybe it's time to cease your complaints about the children He's entrusted to you and start taking care of them before you lose them all."

"Easy for you to say," Dagget sneered.

Pain wrenched through Gabe's heart as he remembered his own childhood. "No, it's not easy for me to say. I understand little Mary's plight." Gabe stood and towered over Dagget. "Look at your daughter. She's not fighting the fever; she has nothing on the inside of her to want to live. Unless you give her a reason, she won't survive."

A bewildered expression spread over the man's face even in his drunken stupor. Gabe turned his attention back to Mary, disgusted at the drunken excuse of a man before him.

"Pray for me, Lena," he whispered. "I'm incensed with Dagget. I think I could tear him apart with my bare hands."

She lifted her gaze from Mary and touched his face. "You're a man who loves his family and doesn't understand why Dagget fails to see his blessings. I'll pray for you and Dagget." She studied Mary's face. "And this poor baby suffering here."

"If only Pa loved her," Amanda softly whispered. "Sometimes we hide her from him so he won't beat her."

"We won't let him hurt her ever again," Charles vowed. He took a deep breath. "I think I'll check on the animals."

Gabe stood. "I'll go with you. Staying inside is making me irritable."

❧

Lena watched Gabe leave, her heart heavy with the sadness etching his features. She wanted to offer comfort, but the right words slipped her mind. Her childhood had been happy and full of wonderful memories, but she'd come to know something terrible had happened to Gabe as a child—something that weighed on him like a heavy yoke. Perhaps she should ask him about it when all of this was over.

She'd never heard Gabe raise his voice, and he really hadn't shouted at Dagget, but his anger had spilled over like a boiling pot. How well she understood the guilt of an uncontrollable temper. Each time she forgot her resolve to contain hers, a matter would irritate her, and her mouth acted before her Christianity set in.

Of course she understood giving it all to God would help, but Lena wanted to end it all on her own—to show God she could please Him. She hadn't been able to curb her unforeseen anger by herself yet. She glanced at Dagget. Drunk. Mean. Hurting those he loved, or should love.

I'm not like him. I'm a good mother and wife. I don't hurt anyone or use horrible language. I love my family, and they love me.

Lena unwillingly recalled the days following James's death when her heart had hardened against God and all those around her, even Caleb and Simon. She'd despised James for leaving her alone to raise two children and manage the farm. Her tears of grief had turned to hate for his abandonment. The turning point came when Caleb asked her why she didn't like him or Simon. Lena had cried and begged God and the boys' forgiveness. Since then, she'd managed her temper fairly well—but not to her satisfaction.

Obviously, Dagget felt the same way about Mary. Unfortunately, he hadn't recognized the poison brewing in his soul.

Lena pushed aside her disturbing thoughts. At present, Mary deserved all of her attention. She bent and kissed the little girl's feverish cheeks. *I'd take this child in a minute— all of them—and give them a proper home where they'd know the meaning of real love.*

"Do you think she will be all right?" Amanda's voice broke into quiet sobs. She sat on the other side of her sister and adjusted the quilt for what seemed like the hundredth time.

"Are you praying?" Lena asked quietly.

Amanda buried her face in her hands. "I don't know what to pray for. I've been Mary's mama since the day she was born, and I love her so very much. I even named her Mary Elizabeth after Ma, but Pa has made her life miserable. Perhaps she should be with Jesus and Mama. At least she'd be happy and loved."

Lena moved alongside the young woman and held her while she wept. "We all want what's best for Mary, and only God in His perfect wisdom knows the answers. He loves her more than we can imagine, and He knows our hearts."

"I want her to fight this and get well," Amanda said, lifting a tear-stained face. "I don't want to lose my little Mary." She turned to the child. "Please get well. I promise to take better care of you. None of us will let you be hurt again."

Lena cried with her. Children shouldn't ever have to suffer for adults' mistakes. "We must pray for God's healing. He can work miracles." Lena took a sideways glance at Dagget, who stared at them. In his slouched position with his chin resting on his chest, huge tears rolled down his face.

"Have I killed my little girl?" he groaned.

Lena recalled Gabe's earlier words. "She needs to hear you love her and want her to live."

Dagget curled his fingers into a ball and trembled. "Amanda," he said softly. "Do we have any coffee?"

"Yes, Pa."

"Would you mind getting me a mug full?"

Amanda tore herself from Lena and brought her father the coffee. Although steam lifted from the hot brew, he downed it quickly. All the while the tears washed over his dirty cheeks. He stared at Mary, wordless. Lena didn't know if his drunkenness had brought on the emotion or if he sincerely regretted the way he'd treated the child.

Mary's breath grew more ragged, and she cried out delirious in her half-conscious state. Lena tried to give her more tea, but the little girl couldn't swallow it.

"Oh, Jesus, please save this precious child," Lena whispered.

An instant later, Dagget scrambled to the floor beside his youngest daughter. He pulled her hand from beneath the quilt and held it firmly. "Mary, I want you to live. I know I've treated you bad, but if you'll give me a chance—if God will give me a chance—I'll make it up to you and your brothers and sisters."

The door squeaked open, and Gabe walked in with Charles. The youth had aged years in a matter of hours. Weariness and a hint of sorrow settled on his features. Gabe's gaze flew to Lena, questioning, wondering, and fearful.

"Charles wants to ride for the doctor, but I've explained the trek is too dangerous with all this snow. As long as there's sunlight, he can find his way, but on a cloudy day, he'll get lost."

Lena nodded in agreement and turned her attention back to Mary. She saw the sorrow on Dagget's face as he held Mary's hand and shed one tear after another. Each time the child coughed, her whole body shook.

"There's a bottle of paregoric under my bed," Dagget said. "Would that help?"

Paregoric. Lena knew it contained opium, and some folks got so they had to have it all the time.

Gabe cleared his throat. "I've heard of its being used for cough before, although its primary use is stomach ailments."

"Would it hurt her?" Amanda asked.

"I knew of a woman who became addicted to laudanum—a mixture of opium and alcohol—but we could try a little of the paregoric," Gabe replied. "It's up to you."

Silence resounded from the walls of the small dugout.

"I think we should try anything that might help," Charles finally said. He ran his fingers through his hair. "We have to do something."

Gabe moved to Dagget's bed and pulled out the small bottle from beneath it. "Let's give her a dose. In the meantime, why don't we call in the other children and pray together for Mary?"

A short while later, they all gathered together while Gabe prayed. "Lord Jesus, all of us have asked You today to spare this child and heal her. Now, we all are praying together. Hear our voices. We look to You for strength. Amen."

&a.

Later that afternoon, with no change in Mary, Gabe realized the necessity of making arrangements for Caleb and Simon. Pulling Lena aside, he shared his thoughts. "The boys ought to get home. I'd like to escort you back. Then I'll return to spend the night here."

"Would you mind if I stayed the night instead?" She stared at the unconscious child, still and dangerously hot. Not once had she left Mary's side with Amanda and Dagget.

"Of course not," he replied. "Whatever happens, Amanda will need you."

She reached for his hand, and he assisted her to her feet. "I'll walk you outside."

While Lena pulled on her coat, Gabe stepped around to Dagget's side. "I'm going home with the boys, but Lena is staying the night."

He nodded. "Uh. . .uh thank you for. . .today. I'll not be forgetting it."

Gabe grasped the man on his shoulder. "I'll be by at daybreak."

Gabe and his family stepped out of the dugout. Once the door shut behind them, Gabe voiced his concerns to Lena. "Do you think Dagget is harmless?"

"Yes, I believe so. Right now regret is eating him alive."

"Do you think it will last?" Gabe remembered all his dealings with Dagget, and the thought of the man tossing his foul words at his precious wife alarmed him.

She shrugged and wrapped her arms around her. "I hope so. These children need him."

"But he's so mean, Mama," Caleb said. "I don't think he'll ever change."

"We have to give him a chance, just like the good Lord does for us," Lena said.

Gabe hugged her and planted a light kiss on her lips. "I love you, Lena Hunters. Now, hurry on inside, before you get too cold."

Caleb and Gabe trudged through the snow back to the farm, while Simon rode the horse. They all were quiet, including Simon, and it offered an opportunity for Gabe to reflect on the Shafers. Oh, how he wanted Mary to live, and how well he understood her desire to die. Children needed love to grow and flourish. Without it, they grew inward, as he'd done. Fortunately for him, he'd come to know a heavenly Father who'd changed his whole life.

"Pa?" Caleb asked.

Gabe gave him his full attention.

"Would you take all six of the Shafers and love them like us?" Caleb asked.

"What do you think?" Gabe responded.

"I believe you would."

"Do you feel my sentiments are wrong?"

Caleb did not hesitate to reply. "No, not at all. I think it's mighty fine."

"Of course, what is best for those children is for their father to love them."

"I'm sure glad we have you for a pa," Simon piped up.

"Me too," Caleb echoed. "We got the best pa in Nebrasky."

❧

Lena had dozed by Mary's side, while Amanda slept off and on. Every time Lena awoke, she saw Dagget staring into his little daughter's face. He didn't eat the supper of salt pork and cornbread that Lena and Amanda prepared and refused anything to drink. The boys did their chores and silently went about their business until time for them to sleep, although Charles sat near the fire, watching Mary. The vigil continued with only the sounds of the younger children's soft snoring and Amanda's quiet weeping.

Just before four o'clock the next morning, Mary stirred. "She feels cooler," Dagget said. "Don't you think so, Lena?"

Immediately, Lena touched the child's forehead. "The fever's broken. Praise God."

Amanda and Charles awakened and scooted closer.

"Mary," Dagget whispered. "Can you talk to me?"

Through half-closed eyes, the child whispered, "I'm so tired."

"Sure you are, Honey. Now you just sleep, and I'll be here when you wake up."

"Are you my Jesus?" Mary asked a moment later.

Dagget sucked in a ragged breath. "It's your pa, Mary. I'm so sorry for being mean to you. I. . .I love you, Child."

Lena blinked back the tears. God had answered many prayers this night. What a dear Lord they served.

sixteen

Lena ladled the freshly churned butter into a small bowl and proceeded to rinse it thoroughly before packing it lightly into a yellow mound. Gabe loved his bread and butter. Even when Caleb and Simon complained about the endless meals of cornbread, Gabe never said a word. Instead, he'd reach for a second hunk. At night, he loved to sit before the fire and feast on leftover cornbread with milk and molasses. Didn't take much to please her husband.

The snow this March came lightly and in inches rather than feet. A few more heavy storms might fall upon them, but the likelihood lessened as the days grew closer to spring. Lena loved the seasons, but she'd had enough of snow and ice.

What a winter, Lena mused, but a much easier one with Gabe to share each day. He'd changed so much since the first time she'd seen him at the train station in Archerville—and not simply in appearance. That alone proved startling enough. He'd shed all the excess weight, and the work outside had tightened his muscles and darkened his skin. One glance at his coppery-colored eyes could leave her breathless, and his thick blond hair, well. . .

In short, Gabe Hunters had transformed into quite a handsome man, but his heart had won hers from the moment he reached out to her and the boys.

I'm a pretty lucky woman to find a man who loves me as much as I do him.

So much had happened in the last month. Dagget had given his permission for Amanda to teach school, and the area farmers had pitched in to make the soddy presentable.

Gabe had offered his assistance in helping Amanda form a schedule and arrange the classes. He'd been guiding her through basic reading, writing, and arithmetic much like she'd done with her brothers.

Today, Gabe had gone hunting while the boys were in school, much to Caleb and Simon's regret. They'd have gladly gone along, skipping their lessons with Amanda in light of a few hours in the wilds. Gabe had taken to regularly bringing in game, and today he had his sights on taking Dagget with him. How strange that these two different men had grown to be such good friends.

"Hello," a voice called.

Lena strained her ears. She didn't recognize the voice. Her sights trailed to the loaded shotgun hanging over the door.

"Hello, Lena?"

She peeked through the window. Dread washed over her.

"Lena!"

She opened the door to see Riley O'Connor dismounting his horse. *Gabe will not be happy about this.* "My husband's not here," she said, crossing her arms.

Riley shot her a wide grin as he tied his mount to the porch post. "I hoped he'd be gone."

"Why?" she snapped. Remembering Riley's temperament when challenged equaled her own, Lena rephrased the question. "I don't understand why you need to see me."

"I think you have a good idea." He loped toward her, offering an easy smile. "I wanted to see you."

She didn't like him, not one bit. "Unless you have business with Gabe, then you don't have any reason to be here."

"You and I have unfinished business," he said low, standing dangerously close.

Lena stepped back and took a deep breath. *Hold your temper. He's bigger than you.* "We have nothing to talk about."

"I asked you to marry me, you refused, and now you're

married to that city feller."

"Then everything is settled." Lena lifted her chin in hopes he understood her silent dismissal.

Riley's eyes narrowed, and he lifted one worn boot onto the porch. "You never gave me a chance."

"For what?"

"To win you back."

"You never had me. Riley, please, just leave. I am a happily married woman. I love my husband very much, and he's going to be upset when he finds out you've been here."

"Good, I'd like the chance to fight 'im."

She closed her eyes and fought for control. Anger bubbled hotter than a pot of lye and tallow. "My Gabe has better things to tend to than fighting you. In case you've forgotten, you and I never courted, never kissed—unlike what you told Gabe—never anything. As I remember, you rode up one day and stated you were planning to marry me. I said no then, and I would say no again, even if you were the last man in the world!"

Riley's foot slipped from the porch, leaving a clump of fresh manure on the edge.

"Aw, Lena, just let me come inside for a spell. I'm sure you'll change your mind."

"Get out of here."

"You're making a terrible mistake. Lots of women think I'm good to look at."

She gritted her teeth. "I don't. Take your charms to one of them."

A wry smile spread over his face. "Why don't we just see?"

Quickly, Lena stepped inside the open door and slammed it. "You best leave, Riley. I have a shotgun in here, and I'm not afraid to use it."

"I'm goin'! I feel sorry for your husband. You ain't worth the trouble."

Latching the door, Lena peeked through the side of her window's calico curtain to watch Riley gallop off. She closed her eyes and touched her pounding heart. *I've got to tell Gabe.*

That evening, while the boys tended to chores and Gabe skinned three rabbits—Dagget had brought down a deer—Lena stole over by the well where Gabe hunched over the animals.

"What's wrong?" he asked, lifting a brow. "You look upset."

She nodded and wrapped her shawl closer about her shoulders.

"It's too cold for you without a coat, Lena. Why don't you stay warm by the fire, and I'll be there momentarily."

"You don't mind?"

He smiled. "I'm finished, and I rather enjoy the opportunity to catch my wife alone."

A few moments later, Gabe joined her at the table. She poured both of them a cup of freshly brewed coffee and sat across from him, her mind spinning with Riley's unpleasant visit. For a few tempting seconds, she thought of not telling him at all. *Who would know the difference? No, that's wrong.*

Taking a deep breath, she blurted out, "Riley O'Connor paid a visit while you were hunting with Dagget." It didn't sound at all as she intended. Trembling, she wrapped her fingers around the mug of hot coffee.

Gabe stared at her—emotionless. "What did he want?"

"He was up to no good, saying things that weren't true."

"What did he want, Lena, and what did he say?"

Suddenly, she burst into tears. "Gabe, if that man ever shows up on our land again, I'm going to fill his backside with buckshot!"

"I'd like to know what happened." The cold tone of Gabe's voice nearly frightened her.

"He just talked about him and me. . .insinuating we used to court. I hurried back into the cabin and told him to leave or I'd get the shotgun after him."

Solemnly, Gabe rose from the table. "I believe I need to pay Mr. O'Connor a visit. I won't have this in my home."

She grabbed his suspenders. "No, Gabe, please. That's what he wants. I told him I was happily married and I loved you." She glanced up at him through blinding tears and repeated the conversation word for word.

Sighing heavily, Gabe lowered himself onto the chair. A distant look filled his eyes, and for a moment, she saw a stranger before her. "I'm glad you told me," he finally said.

"I couldn't keep anything from you. We're supposed to share everything." *This is not like Gabe. If I didn't know better, I'd swear he didn't believe me!*

A shadow of something she didn't recognize swept over his face. "I'm not sure what to do."

"Nothing, Gabe. I really don't think he'll be back. I made him plenty mad."

This time his gaze captured hers, and the grim look changed to the one she cherished. "Let's hope it deterred him, for if there is a next time, I'll be forced to take drastic measures. No one, I repeat, no one will accost my wife."

Lena said nothing as Gabe snatched up his coat from the peg and headed outside. A sick feeling swirled around her stomach. Why did she feel he doubted her?

&

Gabe finished skinning the rabbits with a vengeance that frightened him. Dagget Shafer. Riley O'Connor. How many other men had vied for Lena's attention? Had she encouraged them? Was she still seeing Riley? Why did she have to be so beautiful? He knew the degradation of men when they became consumed by a comely woman. Jealousy enveloped their lives. One sin led to another. Drunkenness. Fights. Murder. Families destroyed and a host of other atrocities.

And I'm traveling down the same highway of destruction.

My jealousy has to cease, or I'll shatter my marriage. He'd fall victim to the same wickedness he'd sworn never to enter. Gabe swiped at a single tear coursing down his cheek. His relationship with Lena ranked second to God. Only a fool would destroy something as good as the Father's gift.

Dropping the knife, he wiped his hands clean on the snow. If only he could eliminate the bitter memories as easily as he'd just washed his hands. Gabe stood and took long strides back to the cabin.

The moment he opened the door, he could see Lena had been weeping. He hated what he saw, knowing his insensitive response had ushered in her tears.

"Lena." He crossed the room and took her into his arms. "I apologize for not understanding how today affected you. All I could dwell on was Riley coming after you."

"You have nothing to be jealous of," she whispered, stroking his cheek and no doubt seeing his single tear. "You are what is most important to me—you and our sons."

He held her against him, his fingers running through her dark silky hair, her breath soft and warm against his neck. "I'm so fortunate to have you in my life. Please forgive me."

"Oh, Gabe. Don't be so hard on yourself. Riley O'Connor is a difficult man. You reacted like any man who'd been insulted."

"It's no excuse for me to be difficult too. We have so many fine friends, and I don't need to make a fuss over one ill-mannered scoundrel."

"I love you, Gabe Hunters. Nothing's going to change my heart."

He held her close, chasing away his fears and bitterness. Someday, he'd have to tell her about Mother and the others, but not now. For this moment, he wanted to simply cherish the woman in his arms.

seventeen

Winter slowly melted into the Platte River, and Gabe eagerly looked forward to spring. At last he could plow the fields and plant corn and other grains for a fall harvest. He wanted to help Lena plant a sizable vegetable garden, knowing she'd have to preserve the food while he worked in the fields. He'd learned so much about Nebraska since last October, and this new season promised to teach him even more. Without a doubt, the cold winter months had given him and his family time to get to know each other. They'd played in the snow, gone hunting, and Lena had taught him how to ice skate.

It has been a good season, he wrote in his journal. *My family is affectionate, and I am deeply grateful for their devotion. I believe we would not have grown this close if the winter had not closed in around us. Now I'm eager to do the work that will provide for my family.*

In the mornings, after milking and chores, Gabe listened for the birds. Through Caleb, he'd learned to distinguish the soft coo of a mourning dove, the unique call of the bobwhite, the obnoxious cry of the crow, and from time to time, the gobble of a turkey, which reminded him of chattering women. Near the river, ducks and geese abounded, and occasionally, he and the boys would bring one down for a fine meal.

Once he'd sowed the crops, Gabe wanted to take Caleb and Simon fishing. Of course, the first few times the boys would have to teach him how to properly operate a pole, line, and bait. No doubt, he'd provided yet another source of amusement—but he didn't mind.

Dagget and his family worked through their differences.

Little Mary never left her father's side, nor did he object. Dagget had even bought a cow, which ended Gabe's morning visits. Still, a few times a week, Gabe ventured toward the Shafer farm just to keep his mind at ease. Shoots of spring plants weren't the only things thriving at the Shafers.

Lena and the boys had shown Gabe how to read the tracks of the white-tailed deer, coyotes, foxes, rabbits, and a host of other animals. He looked forward to seeing prairie dogs, for Simon found them quite interesting.

The wolves hadn't bothered them since the incident with Caleb and Simon, although Gabe still looked for them from time to time. He'd lost a few head of cattle over the winter: three to hungry wolves, two others to the cold.

Gabe wouldn't trade his new life for the biggest mansion in Philadelphia—or anywhere else for that matter. Being a husband, father, and farmer surely must be God's richest blessing.

Today, he'd begin the plowing. Like a child eagerly awaiting a spectacular event, Gabe hadn't been able to sleep all night.

"Gabe, it's hard work," Lena warned. "Your shoulders will ache. In fact, your whole body will hurt. You'll fall into bed dead tired only to get up before dawn and start again. I think I should help, Caleb too."

"Maybe Caleb—later," Gabe replied with a frown. "But not my wife. I'm the provider."

Before the sun offered a faint twinge of pink, Gabe hurried through his chores, then hitched up the mule to the iron plow. He slipped the reins over his shoulders and offered a quick prayer. Grinning like a love-struck schoolboy, he took out across the earth, all the while envisioning fields of waving corn and grain just like he'd seen in his books.

After one length of a field, Gabe realized the truth in Lena's words. Plowing was hard work! He looked behind him and saw his beloved wife watching. Waving wildly, he gestured to the completed row. Turning the mule, he began again. No point in letting her know she'd spoken correctly in her assessment of the plowing.

Tonight he'd be one sore man.

Midmorning, Lena brought a crockery jug of cold water wrapped in burlap and a cloth to wipe the sweat from his brow.

"Admit it, Gabe. This is hard work," she said while he drank deeply.

Not yet, maybe never.

When he refused to reply, she laughed. "I'm sure your books on farming didn't talk about the sweat pouring off your face or the way your back feels like it's breaking in two."

He tried to give her a stern look, but one glimpse of her sweet face melted his resolve. "The endeavor is satisfying," he said, clamping on his lip so she wouldn't hear his chuckle.

"Are you ready for me to help? Or can I send the boys as soon as they get home from school?"

"No, Ma'am. I'm a Nebraska farmer, and I'm excited about plowing my own fields."

"And you're sure about this? Caleb will be disappointed since he wanted to help."

He leaned over and kissed her. "I made it through the fall and winter—wolves, Dagget, blizzards, and Riley. Now I'm ready for the spring and summer and whatever comes with it."

She wrapped her arms around his neck. "Tornadoes. We get some nasty twisters in the summer. Prairie fires too." She tilted her head. "Back in '73, we had a horrible drought, and in '74 the worst plague of grasshoppers ever seen—ate everything to the ground. Even the trains couldn't run because the tracks were slick with 'hoppers."

"I'm ready." He grinned.

"I see you are." She stepped back from his embrace and

laughed with him. "I'll bring you food and water in a few hours. Besides, you're beginning to smell like a farmer."

By noon, Gabe wondered how many days it would take to complete the plowing. It had taken him half a day to till one acre. No doubt by the time he finished, he'd be strong and muscular. He grimaced at the mere thought of Lena guiding the plow over the rough terrain and supporting the reins. No woman should work like a man.

After devouring dandelion greens and cornbread at noon, Gabe fought the urge to stretch out on the blanket where Lena had set their meal and sleep a few moments before submitting himself to the plow again.

I am a farmer. We don't shirk in our work.

"Close your eyes for a little while," she urged, coaxing him to lay his head on her lap. "The plowing doesn't have to be finished today, and you were out here before the sun barely peeked through the clouds."

"Now I understand how Samson felt," he said. "Next you will want to know where I confine my strength."

She stroked his cheek with her fingertips. Intoxicating.

"I'm a farmer, not a lazy city man," he mumbled. "I'm going to call you Delilah."

She combed her fingers through his hair; soon her touch faded into memory.

&

Lena woke with a start. She'd fallen asleep! She'd planned for Gabe to rest before finishing the day's work. Shielding her eyes from the sun, she saw him in the distance struggling with the mule. Why, he'd gotten so much done. How long had she slept? From the sun's position in the sky, she must have napped for over an hour.

"Gabe Hunters, you tricked me!"

He heard her call and took a moment to wave. She wanted to shout at him, but the incident suddenly struck her as funny.

Looking about, she saw he'd gathered up the remains of their meal and packed it nicely into the basket. Only the quilt beneath her needed to be folded and placed with the other items.

"Gabe Hunters, you never cease to surprise me," she whispered. Beneath her fair-haired husband's smile and gentle ways rested more courage and grit than any man around. *He's a warrior,* she thought. *The best there is.*

Humming a nondescript tune, she walked back to the house. The boys should be home from school by now and seeking out mischief if she guessed correctly. Perhaps her strong-willed husband would accept Caleb's help.

As darkness covered the farm and stars dotted the sky, Gabe came trudging in for supper with Caleb and Simon behind him. Although they'd washed at the well and their cheeks glistened from the scrubbing, the lines in their faces and their hunched backs betrayed their exhaustion.

"I have beef stew," she said brightly, "and a dried choke-berry pie with fresh cream."

"I'm starved," Simon moaned, dropping into a chair.

"I don't know why," Caleb said with a glare. "All afternoon you and Turnip chased rabbits, while Pa and I took turns at the plow."

"You didn't work that much," Simon replied. "I saw Pa do more rows than you."

Mercy, let's not argue. Gabe is tired enough without settling the boys.

Gabe ruffled Caleb's hair. "You both worked equally hard, and you spent a good part of the day in school. Caleb, you were a great help in the fields, and Simon, thank you for completing the evening chores without assistance."

"Why don't we eat so you men can get to bed," Lena said, filling their plates with the hot stew and a slab of buttered cornbread.

"It smells delicious," Gabe said. He chewed slowly as

though every motion took all of his strength. "Do you boys mind if I postpone our reading of *The Last of the Mohicans* until tomorrow night?"

Caleb sighed. "I'm too tired to listen."

Simon agreed.

Shortly thereafter, the two boys went to bed with promises to say their prayers before drifting off to sleep. "School is just too hard for me," Simon said.

Lena captured Gabe's gaze and smiled. Their youngest son was not about to admit the afternoon's venture had worn him out. She watched the two boys disappear into their small room.

Gabe slumped into a chair, and she immediately stepped behind him, massaging the shoulder muscles she knew were tight and sore. He winced. "And so what has made you so tired?" she whispered.

He pulled her around and down onto his lap, offering a light kiss. "All the good food I ate today. Plowing is fairly simple."

She shook her head. "I suppose the pain I detect is a bee sting?" she asked with a tilt of her head and a smile she could not hide.

"Not exactly." Gabe tossed her a most pathetic look, reminding her of a little boy seeking sympathy.

"Is that the way you peered at your mother when you needed something?" Lena asked, pretending to be stern.

Immediately, Gabe stiffened. *What have I done?* She knew he never spoke of his mother, except to discourage a conversation.

"Maybe I should go to bed."

Lena despised her foolishness. "I'm sorry. I know you don't like to talk about your mother."

He gently lifted her from his lap. "It's all right. My mother behaved rather uniquely with her maternal instincts."

"She really hurt you," Lena stated, wanting to touch him

but slightly fearful. The regret and anger in his face had only occurred once before—when he'd dealt with Dagget Shafer the night Mary nearly died.

Shrugging, he chewed at his lip. "I'm a grown man with a fine family. I determined a long time ago to rise above my circumstances. Revisiting the past is pointless." He stood and grasped her arms. She could feel him trembling. "Lena, I don't want to speak of my mother ever again. She's buried, and everything about her is best forgotten."

"I'd be glad to listen. It might help how you feel."

"No!"

eighteen

Lena woke the following morning to discover Gabe had already left for the fields. She'd slept soundly, not her normal manner of doing things, but she'd had a difficult time falling asleep the night before. She'd cried before coming to bed, and not once had Gabe apologized or attempted to hold her when she crawled in beside him. This morning she was furious.

When she finally climbed out of bed, she discovered Caleb and Simon were outside doing their morning chores before school, and she hadn't prepared their breakfast or lunch buckets. Even with time pressing against her, the memory of Gabe's final words last night seared her heart.

Slapping together cornbread and molasses sandwiches, Lena roughly wrapped the lunches in a cloth and tossed it into the boys' buckets. She turned her attention to the boys' breakfast. Anger raced through her veins as she heated the skillet for fried cornmeal and eggs. *Look at all I've done for him, and this is how he treats me! Where would he be if I hadn't married him and taught him about farming?*

Without warning, Lena felt her stomach roll. *Now, look what Gabe's done—made me sick with his rudeness.*

Who has made you ill?

The gentle whisper penetrated her soul. She'd allowed her temper to upset her, the evil poison she'd sworn to overcome. Gabe had nothing to do with her churning stomach. Pulling the skillet from the fire, she dashed outside to rid her body of whatever had revolted in her stomach. Sick and feeling the pain of remorse, Lena realized she couldn't go on with the rage inside her.

After the boys left for school, Lena picked up the Bible. Oh, how she needed the Lord this day. Every part of her wanted to crumble in memory of her horrible temper. She remembered her thoughts the day when Mary hovered between life and death and how Dagget's ugly temperament had nearly killed the child. *Am I any different? Would I lose Gabe and the boys if they knew the horrible things I was thinking?*

Praise God, Gabe and her sons had been outside and not witnessed her tantrum. The One who really counted, the One she'd given her life to had heard every thought and seen every deed. Lena rubbed her arms; the guilt of her sin made her feel dirty. She thought she could resolve her temper without bothering God. One more time she'd failed. How long before she destroyed the affections of her family with her selfishness?

Opening the Bible, she leafed through page after page, reading the notes and underlined passages. Some Scripture she had marked, others came from Gabe or James. Remembrances of all the nights by the fire listening to her husband read and pray settled upon her as though she'd crawled up into God's lap.

Choking back her tears, Lena continued turning the pages of the Bible, allowing His Word to soothe her troubled spirit. The book of Romans graced her fingers; the first verse of chapter eight she had memorized as a girl: "There is therefore now no condemnation to them which are in Christ Jesus, who walk not after the flesh, but after the Spirit."

But I am walking after the flesh by not turning over my anger to the Lord. My rebellion is displeasing to the One who has given me life.

Catching her breath, Lena shivered. How could she expect to please God on her own? She must give Him her struggles at this very moment.

Heavenly Father, You have blessed me far more than I could ever imagine. I'm sorry for not giving You my problem with anger. In the whole six months Gabe and I have been married, not once has he ever raised his voice or initiated an argument. It's always been me. Take this burden from me, I pray, for without You, I will only sin more and more. Amen.

Closing the Bible and laying it on the table, she proceeded to tidy up from breakfast. Peace lifted her spirit. No longer did she feel sick or angry, but instead, she prayed about the problems plaguing Gabe with his mother. The woman must have hurt him deeply for him not to want her mentioned. Poor Gabe. Such a good, sweet man. He'd given her, Caleb, and Simon his devotion without asking for anything in return.

With a new resolve to live every moment of her life totally for her Father, Lena determined to never confront Gabe with any questions about his past. Let him come to her if he desired to talk. Until then, she'd pray for peace in his soul.

At noon she carried a basket of cornbread, newly churned butter, apple butter, boiled eggs, and a slab of ham along with a jug of buttermilk and another one of water to the fields. Gabe must be starved by now. They'd fared well during the winter with plenty of food—although they'd all gotten tired of cornmeal and molasses. With spring here, she could gather fresh greens, elderberries, and chokeberries. Later on in the summer, fresh vegetables would add variety to their diets. And as always, everything would be dried for the next winter.

❧

During the morning, Gabe had plowed with a vengeance, completing more rows than he thought possible. Dagget said the corn should be planted by the twentieth of May to insure its being knee-high by July fourth. At this rate, he'd be done with time to spare.

All the while he deliberated on the way he'd spoken to Lena the previous night. She meant nothing by her innocent remark, and he'd lashed out at her unfairly. If he admitted the truth, Lena should be told about his mother. The woman who had given him birth might have gone to her grave, but the wounds still drew blood. Not a day went by that he didn't ponder over something she'd said or done. This pattern of action made him think he hadn't truly forgiven her.

Lena had allowed God to work through her. She said and did the right things to instill self-confidence in everything he did. Every day he looked forward to what God had planned for him and his family. Lena loved him, and he loved her. The doubts he'd experienced in the beginning about her fidelity grew less and less as he viewed her true spirit. She trusted him, and he needed to trust her.

Gabe chuckled despite his grievous thoughts. His Lena had a temper. Feisty, that one. She'd warned him repeatedly about her outbursts, but he hadn't seen much of them. He enjoyed her free spirit. *I bet she's boiling over this morning.* The thought saddened him. Any repercussion from last night clearly was his fault.

He must apologize, but in doing so he had to reveal the truth of his past. *Can I tell a portion of my life without revealing the entire story?* The answer came as softly as the breeze cooling his tired face. Truth didn't mean dissecting what he comfortably could and could not state.

Gabe stretched his neck and stared at the sun straight up in the sky. Glancing toward the house, he saw Lena edging toward him, carrying a basket. Bless her. He didn't deserve her bringing him food. An urgency knocked at his heart.

Lord, I'm afraid I haven't given You the past—not completely. I realize now if I had allowed You to share my pain, I would have been able to tell Lena about Mother. Take the bitterness from me and use my past to Your glory.

Shifting the reins around his shoulders and giving Turnip a pat, he proceeded to plow the row that brought him closer to his wife. Suddenly, the burden didn't seem so heavy.

Lena and Gabe met at the end of the row—she with her

basket of food and he wearing an apology on his lips. Halting the mule, he dropped the leather pieces to his side and approached her. She wore a timid smile, a quivering smile. He felt lower than the dirt he plowed to submission beneath his feet.

"Lena," he said, "I apologize for the way I spoke to you last night, and in my self-pity, I neglected to tell you good night or kiss you properly."

She nibbled at her lip. "Would you like to kiss me now?"

"I smell of sweat and the mule."

"That's a farmer's smell." Lena offered a half smile. "I love my farmer." She set the basket onto the ground and reached out for him.

Gabe enveloped her in his arms, and she clung to him as though they'd been apart for days. He bent to claim her lips, tenderly at first, then more fervently than their first night together. At last, he drew himself back. "I never meant to hurt you. You are the sunshine to me each morning and the vivid colors of sunset each night."

"I wish I could state things as wonderfully as you," she whispered. "You make me feel special—pretty and pleasing."

"And you are; you always will be."

Her shoulders fell, and she shook her head. "I'm sorry for all the wicked things I thought about you," she whispered. "And the things I threw."

He could not disguise his smile. "What did you throw?"

She swallowed hard. "A ham bone, but I picked it up and brought it for Turnip."

Gabe roared with laughter.

"No, please," she said, her eyes misting. "You don't understand. That bone is what brought about my prayer giving God my horrible temper." She stared up at him. "I did it, Gabe. I surrendered my anger to the Lord."

Once more pulling her close, he realized he had not been

the only one to confess sin this day. "His ears must be filled with the Hunters from Nebraska. The Lord and I had a talk of our own."

She waited patiently, a look of curiosity and love glowing from the luminous green pools of her eyes.

He lifted the basket. "Let's eat, and I will tell you all about it."

The food tasted wonderful, and the talk between them was light and flirtatious. Gabe knew he masked the serious conversation about to evolve, but the Lord promised to be his strength.

"Are you ready to hear a story?" he asked, wiping a spot of apple butter from Lena's lip.

"I always like a good story."

"This one has a remarkable ending."

"I'm ready, Gabe, for whatever you want to tell me."

He nodded and lifted his gaze to the heavens for a quick prayer before he began with the story only his heavenly Father knew. "My mother never knew my father. She worked at a brothel in Philadelphia. . .an exquisite woman whose parents were from Norway. I remember she had hair the color of the sun and eyes the fairest of blue, but her disposition didn't match." He paused, and Lena reached over to take his hand.

"Mother gave me the last name of Hunters, although I have no idea where she found it. I was an inconvenience and an irritation to her. . .well, her business transactions. At an early age, she left me alone while she worked. She drank to drown her own pain, which only made her even more disagreeable. She took her disappointments with life out on me, and so did many of the gentlemen she brought home. I quickly became their whipping boy. The tongue-lashings and beatings were unbearable until I learned to believe I deserved them for whatever reason they gave me." Gabe covered the hand touching his. "I know you've seen the scars on my back, and I thank you for not mentioning them before."

Huge tears rolled down her cheeks, and he hastily added, "Don't cry. This has a happy ending, remember?" With a deep breath he continued. "As I grew older, I became absorbed with learning. School was the perfect diversion for the abuse at home. However, when the other students discovered where I lived and what my mother did, I became the brunt of their ridicule. So I buried myself even deeper into my books. I grew infatuated with words. Their meanings gave me power, and that's when I started using them to fight back. No one else might have comprehended their meanings, but I did. It gave me an opportunity to consider myself better than the ones who shunned me.

"About the time I turned sixteen, Mother purchased the brothel and became the madam of the largest establishment of its type in Philadelphia. She enlisted me to work there, do her books, and keep her records straight. Also at the same age, I received a Bible from a well-meaning group of ladies from a nearby church who aspired to reform everyone living within the confines of the brothel. The women didn't want the book, so I began reading it." He paused, and she said nothing, as if knowing he would continue.

"Shortly thereafter, I started attending church. No one knew or cared, for they were all sleeping off the escapades from the night before.

"When I turned twenty, Mother developed a cough. The doctors couldn't find a cure. Her only temporary relief came from medication that she began to rely on as much as the alcohol. Remember when Dagget asked about giving little Mary paregoric, and I told him about the woman who became addicted to laudanum? That was Mother. By the time I reached thirty, she had to be nursed day and night."

"And you took care of her?" Lena asked.

"Yes. She depended solely on me. I resented it at first, but the Lord kept dealing with me until I forgave her—at least I thought I did. But the bitterness stayed with me." He squeezed her hand. "That's why becoming a husband and father meant so much to me. I had to make up for what had been done to me."

Lena nodded, the tears glistening on her face. He brushed them aside. "I understand, Gabe. I really do. You are a wonderful father."

"But a true miracle happened right here on this farm—the blessings of love. You have no idea of the joy that filled my soul the first time Caleb and Simon called me Pa. I would have died a happy man right then. But your love has been the finest treasure of all. God gave me all these gifts, but I could not release my resentment until this morning." He reached up to touch her cheek. "And my story has such a beautiful ending. I have the richest of blessings at my fingertips."

nineteen

Lena wept with Gabe until they began to tease each other about their puffy and reddened eyes. *We are a pair, Gabe Hunters, you and I.*

"You look like you've been in a fight and lost," Lena accused, blowing her nose on his clean handkerchief—one of the items from Philadelphia that he still insisted upon carrying.

He lifted a brow. "And who rammed their fist into your face, Miss Blow-Your-Nose-Like-a-Honking-Goose?"

She wiggled her shoulders to feign annoyance. "My nose, Sir? I thought we were talking about your eyes. Maybe Turnip threw the punches."

He drew her into his arms and kissed the tip of her nose. "Promise me we will always have laughter," he whispered. "I want us to talk, to cry together, even to argue from time to time, and always to laugh."

Laughter. Yes, what a true blessing. He'd never laughed so much in his entire life.

"I'll do my best," she said with a smile. "You are much more handsome with a smile on your face." She took a deep breath. "Although today was necessary too."

"I agree," he replied. "I'm insistent about urging the boys and you to discuss your thoughts and feelings, but I'm not always so quick to adhere to the same advice."

"I really am sorry for your unhappy childhood," Lena said seriously. "We had our good times and bad, but my memories are sweet."

He stared at the fields, the cabin, and back to her. "When

147

I reflect on it, I can't help but see the good resulting from those days."

"You mean your compassion for people? For children?"

"Yes. I could have easily drifted into Mother's manner of living and not come to know God."

"Did she ever accept Jesus as her Savior?"

He picked up a clod of dirt and sent it soaring across the plowed field. "I don't know if she ever asked Him to rule her life or not. I talked to her about the Lord and read to her from the Bible, but I never knew if she actually made a decision."

Silence held them captive. Lena felt eternally grateful for the day. They'd both shed ugly garments that not only threatened their relationship with the Lord but also their happiness as husband and wife.

"I have something else to tell you," Gabe said. "I hope when I've finished you won't feel I have deceived you in any way."

She stared at him curiously.

"Mother died a wealthy woman, which meant I inherited the brothel and an exorbitant amount of money. I dissolved the business, in case you wondered." He glanced teasingly at her. "And I donated the building to a church, which now uses it as an orphanage. After praying through what God wanted me to do with the rest of the funds, I gave to several churches and deposited the balance in a Philadelphia bank. When the time comes, we will be able to provide funds for Caleb and Simon's education. There is plenty there to expand the farm when we're ready and for other unforeseen expenses. Someday, I'd like to take you on a trip, anywhere you want to venture."

Lena felt the color drain from her face. "Why ever would you want a poor widow when you could have had so much more?"

"God had a plan, Dearest. A very pleasant one, I might add. However, I do believe I gained more than money from my adventure in Nebraska."

"I'm so very lucky," she whispered.

He gave her the smile meant only for her. "Nonsense. I am the fortunate man."

My dear, sweet husband. You try so hard. "Want to know my thoughts and feelings right now?" she asked.

"Most certainly."

She closed her eyes. "I want a kiss, a very nice long one."

"I can oblige."

"Not just right now, Gabe. I want one every day for the rest of our lives."

"I can still oblige."

"Even if we've quarreled or the things around us threaten our joy in the Lord and in each other?" she asked, tracing his lips with her fingertip. "No matter if snow blizzards keep us inside for days, or rain forgets to fall, or grasshoppers eat the very clothes we wear, or Caleb and Simon disappoint us?"

"I promise to oblige."

"Good, let's begin now."

&

"How far is this town you're talking about?" Gabe asked, teasing Caleb and Simon about the three-mile walk to see a prairie dog town. They'd gone to church earlier, and the boys had been pestering him for days to visit this spot. "Is there a hotel? A sheriff? I'm really thirsty too."

Lena giggled. He glanced her way as they walked and captured a loving gaze. She still looked pale from being ill that morning, but the color had returned to her cheeks. She'd been perfectly fine the night before. The idea of his precious wife—or any of his family—falling prey to one of the many illnesses tearing through this land alarmed him. He squeezed her hand, sending love messages from his heart to hers.

A year ago he'd received her first letter. So much had happened since then. God had transformed him into a new man, taken away his selfishness, and worked continually to mold him into a godly husband and father. *Thank You, God, for the gift of family and their love.*

"It's not much farther, Pa," Caleb said. "We have to be quiet because once they sense we're around, they stop chattering and disappear."

"And what do they say?" Gabe asked. "Don't believe I've ever had a conversation with a prairie dog."

Simon frowned and shook his head. "You don't understand what they're saying; you just know they're talking to each other."

Lena nibbled at her lip, no doubt to keep from laughing. "Simon, why don't you tell him what they look like?"

"That's right. I haven't seen a good picture in one of my books." Gabe grinned. "Are they as big as Turnip?"

"No, Sir," Simon replied. "Be glad we left him at home 'cause he'd scare them down into their holes."

"They live in holes? I thought they lived in a town."

Simon shook his head in what appeared to be exasperation. "Prairie dogs are smaller than rabbits. They live under the ground, but we call them towns. When you see them, they sit on their back legs and wave their front legs like arms. Then they talk to each other. Remember how Miss Nettie Franklin used her arms when she talked that Sunday in church about drinking whiskey being a sin?"

How well I remember. I thought Judge Hoover would burst since he owns the town's saloon. "She was quite demonstrative that day and quite successful in gaining everyone's attention."

"Gabe," Lena whispered. "Let's not encourage Simon."

He winked at his wife. "Go ahead, Simon."

"Well, that's how those prairie dogs look when they are talking to each other, flapping their arms as if they are pointing out something that really matters."

"Hush, Simon," Caleb said. "We're almost there, and I don't

want Pa to miss them."

The four moved ahead, being careful not to make a sound. In the distance, Gabe heard chattering—like a squirrel convention. As he inched closer with his family right beside him, he saw the humorous stance of the peculiar animals. They *did* resemble Nettie, and he stifled a laugh. What a town indeed!

Suddenly, the animated creatures detected humans and dived into their burrowed homes. Nothing remained but the doorways into their dwellings.

"Doesn't appear to be a good town to ride through," Gabe remarked a short time later, "especially if your horse stepped through one of those holes."

"True," Lena replied. "Of course there are a few people towns too dangerous for decent folk to walk through too."

"Is my philosophical nature rubbing off on you, Dear?" Gabe asked, slipping his hand from hers to wrap around her waist.

"Oh no," Simon moaned. "Does that mean Ma is going to start using all those big words too?"

"I might," she said with a tilt of her head. "Do you mind?"

The little boy's eyes widened, and he stared at his brother. "What do you think, Caleb?"

"Might be all right. Ma could take over teaching school for Amanda." His eyes sparkled mischievously, so much like his mother.

"That wouldn't do at all," Simon quickly replied. "Pa needs her at home. She wouldn't be happy teaching school, and then she'd be too tired to cook supper."

"And I'd miss her," Gabe added. "Amanda will have to keep the job until the town finds someone else."

twenty

Gabe stared up at the sky. Black clouds swirled, and the rumble of distant thunder with a flash of lightning intensified nature's threat. Storms and high winds he could handle, and he'd learned that when it rained, the household items had to be shifted from one side of the cabin to the other—depending on the direction of the rainfall. But the green color spreading across the horizon bothered him.

Glancing at the barn anchored deep into the earth, he wondered if Lena and the boys would be safer there than in the soddy. Although the walls of their home were nearly three feet thick, a twister could still do a lot of damage.

With a heavy sigh, he wished Caleb and Simon were home from school. He focused his attention to the east, straining to see if they were heading this way. Nothing. A gust of wind nearly toppled him over. *This is not merely prairie winds, but a malevolent act of nature.*

Gabe wondered if he should set the mule and horses free to run with the cattle until after the storm, but if his family were safer in the barn, then those animals would be as well. The cattle were contained in barbed-wire fencing. Of course that could be easily blown down.

With a heavy sigh, he realized they'd had a good spring. The corn stood more than a foot high, and they'd been blessed with ample rain. He hadn't considered he might lose a crop. Suddenly, all those days of work twisted through him. Lena's words about the Lord providing for their needs echoed through his ears.

This spring, tornadoes had always managed to venture far

from them—until now.

Drenched in sweat, he stepped outside and studied the southwest sky. In a matter of minutes, the temperatures had dropped, and the wind had increased its velocity. *Where were Caleb and Simon?* Then he saw his sons racing home against a background of a hideous green sky. The closer they came, the better he felt.

Thank You, Lord. I didn't mind You taking care of them, but I feel much better knowing where they are.

"Gabe," Lena called from the doorway. "This looks bad, and I'm worried about the boys."

"They're coming," he replied above the wind. "I see them. Are we safer in the barn?"

"I think so." She scanned the sky, then shouted, "Hurry!" to Caleb and Simon, although Gabe doubted the boys could hear their mother's call. By the time they'd all scurried into the barn, huge droplets of rain pelted the earth. Ear-splitting cracks of thunder resounded, and jagged streaks of lightning split the sky.

"I saw a twister touch down in the distance," Caleb managed to say, trying to catch his breath. "Looked to be heading this way."

Gabe skirted his family to the farthest corner of the barn cradled deep into the hill. He positioned the horses and mule in front of them in case of flying debris. The structure had been built facing the east, which gave him some comfort in their safety. He moved to the opening, seeking some sign of the twister. "It might miss us," he said, watching the wind tug at the roof of the cabin.

"We'll know soon enough," Lena shouted. "Gabe, please don't stand out there. You don't have any idea how the wind could snatch you up."

"I'm being careful." His gaze fixed southwest to where a dark funnel cloud moved their way. The fury of nature left him in awe. One minute it showered his crops with water and in the next it threatened to beat them to the ground.

As the twister soared across the fields, a roar, like the bellowing of a huge beast, sent a tingle from his neck to his spine. This was not a time to stand outside and challenge the wind. Foolishness invited a loss of life—his own.

"Gabe!" Lena called frantically.

"I'm coming," he replied, moving back.

Huddled against his family, Gabe listened to the creature spin closer. "I hope all of you are praying," he said. "Not only for us, but for others in the twister's path."

They didn't reply. His request didn't warrant one. In the shadows, he couldn't see the emotion on their faces, but from the way Lena, Caleb, and Simon trembled beneath his arms, he knew fright penetrated their bones.

"Aren't you afraid, Pa?" Simon whispered shakily.

"Of course I am. But God is in control, and at times like these we have to hold onto our faith."

"Wish I could see Him," Caleb said.

"You can, Son. God's in the quiet summer day, the blizzards last winter, and in the wind outside. Close your eyes, and you can feel Him wrapping His love around you."

Lena squeezed his hand, and he brushed a kiss across her cheek. "I love you," she said. "Seems like you always say the right things to make us feel better."

He forced a chuckle. "I'll remember that the next time I slip and use those long words you so despise."

A deafening crash of thunder caused Simon to jump and snuggle closer. "If I had known we all were going to be this close, I'd have taken my bath before Saturday night," Gabe said.

Caleb giggled. *Thank You, Lord, for Your comfort. Keep us in the shelter of Your wings. Peace, be still. Amen.*

As ferocious as the storm sounded, the wind finally ceased to howl and left only a steady fall of rain in its wake. Gabe released his family. He was grateful they were unharmed. Now he needed to see what had been done outside. Swallowing hard, he made his way to the front of the barn. Although the rain had continued to fall, the cabin stood with only minor roof damage. He glanced to the fields surrounding them. They looked untouched except for one in the direct path of the tornado. The corn planted there bent to the ground as if paying homage to a wicked wind god, but perhaps the stalks might right themselves in the next few days. Even if that didn't happen and the field of corn perished, they'd survive.

Sometimes he thought his optimism masked good sense, but he always tried to buffer his decisions with logic. Leading his family was often. . .

Gabe searched for the proper word. Glancing back at the boys, he knew exactly what fit. Hard. Just plain hard. What a relief to know God held the world in the palm of His hand.

He felt Lena touch his shoulder. "Do you suppose we should check on the Shafers?"

He nodded. "I also need to make sure the cattle fared well, but I can do that on the way there. Any chance of the twister changing directions and heading back this way?"

She sighed. "Doubtful, though I've seen two touch down in the same day."

"We'll wait until the sky clears." He clasped the hand on his shoulder. "The Shafers' dugouts are in bad shape. I know Dagget plans to build a soddy once harvest is over."

"Amanda told me. She's very excited. Dugouts don't last much longer than seven years, and Dagget built that one ten years ago."

"Sure hope the twister didn't step up his plans," Gabe said, glancing at the distant sky in the Shafers' direction. It looked menacing in a mixture of navy and green.

❧

The tornado had laid waste to the dugouts and fencing of

Dagget's farm. From what Gabe could tell, the wind had hit them as if they were a child's toys.

"Hello!" he called, stepping down from the wagon. "Dagget, it's Gabe and Lena and the boys."

A pool of water streaming from the door indicated the inside trench used to keep out the abundance of water had overflowed. What a mess for them to endure.

The door swung open, and Amanda stepped out along with some of her brothers and Mary. "We're all right," she called, "but Pa and Charles rode out this morning to check on fences and haven't returned."

Gabe's insides twisted with fear. He didn't like the sound of those two out in that storm. Dagget had changed considerably since their first encounter. He'd become a caring man and wouldn't endanger his family. "Which way did they go, Amanda?"

She pointed to the southwest. "That way."

Lena nudged him. He hadn't noticed when she'd climbed down from the wagon. "I'll stay and see what I can do here. Why don't you go look for them?"

Their gazes met. She obviously felt the same concern he did. "The wagon might be necessary," he said.

She nodded, her thoughts evident in the lines of her face. "Do you want to take Caleb?"

Gabe studied the growing boy, now twelve years old. In some cultures he'd be considered a man. Still, he'd like to shelter him for as long as possible from the ugliness of the world.

"I'd like to go, Pa," Caleb said. "I'm nearly as tall as you, and I could help."

Placing a hand on the boy's shoulder, Gabe silently agreed. Life's lessons could be a difficult lot, but he'd rather they occur while Caleb was with him than for the boy to learn on his own.

The sheared path before them looked like someone had

taken a razor to the field. To the right, barbed wire stood untouched. Cattle grazed peacefully on their left.

"Do you suppose Mr. Shafer and Charles are dead?" Caleb asked as the wagon ambled on.

Gabe's heart plummeted. "I don't know, Son, but we'll deal with whatever we find. Dagget and Charles know this country, and I'm sure they read the signs of the twister."

"I remember when my first pa died," Caleb went on. "He just went to sleep and didn't wake up."

I hope if God has taken them home, we don't find their bodies mangled. A vision of the wolves crossed his mind. He had the rifle. By now the sun shone through the clouds, and the sky gave no hint of rain or the earlier violence. Calm. Peaceful.

Within the hour, Gabe spotted Charles on the trodden grass, bending over his father. "I believe we've found them," he said, breaking the silence.

"Mr. Shafer must be hurt," Caleb said. "Sure hope he's all right."

Gabe merely nodded. Charles had not moved, and he surely had seen and heard the approaching wagon. Once Gabe pulled it to a halt, Charles lifted a tear-stained face.

"Pa's gone," he said with a heavy sigh. "We tried to outrun the twister. I didn't know he'd fallen."

Gabe surmised what else had happened. "Are you hurt?"

"No, Sir."

"Can I take a look at your pa?"

Charles swallowed hard. "When I looked back, the twister had picked him up. Then it slammed him into the ground. I thought it had knocked the breath out of him, but his head hit hard."

As Charles moved aside, Gabe saw the blood rushing from Dagget's crown. "Caleb, stay in the wagon for now."

From the looks of him, Dagget had died from the blows to

his head. Charles dried his eyes, and together the two lifted Dagget into the back of the wagon while Caleb minded the horses.

Charles said nothing as they drove back to his home. Sorrow etched his young face. Upon sight of his family's farm, he finally spoke. "He's been a good pa since last winter. Before that, I don't know if I'd have grieved so much."

"Now you have good memories," Gabe replied softly.

"I want to bury him beside Ma. He missed her terribly."

"I understand. We'll get the minister and have a proper burial."

Charles wiped his nose with his shirtsleeve. "Thank you, Mr. Hunters. You're a good neighbor."

Gabe startled at the sight of the minister already there when they arrived. He'd ridden out once the twister blew through.

Odd. Why here at the Shafers? Gabe wondered until he saw the way the man looked at Amanda.

"I should have guessed the reverend would be riding out to check on things," Charles said. "He's taken a fancy to Amanda."

God had already made provision for the Shafers. It appeared to him that Jason Mercer needed that family as much as they needed him.

"Glad you had the foresight to come," Gabe said, shaking the reverend's hand.

"I couldn't let a moment pass without riding out," he replied. "I had a notion something was wrong."

The following morning, Gabe, Charles, and Caleb dug the grave for Dagget. The ceremony was short but meaningful to his family. Dagget had died a good man, filling his life with the things that mattered most—God and his family. Little Mary plucked some goldenrods and laid them atop the mound of dirt.

"For you, Pa," she whispered. "I'll always love you."

Lena edged closer to Gabe and took his hand. He felt her body shudder. For the first time he understood why she fretted over him and the boys. Love didn't stop death, it simply made it harder to say good-bye.

Gabe dipped his pen in the inkwell and wrote his reflections about the tornado, then ended his entry with Dagget's death.

Dagget was a good friend. Although we didn't start out this way, the Lord saw fit to bring us together. Lena believes Dagget learned a lot from me, but the truth is he taught me a few valuable lessons. Aside from hunting techniques, which I sorely needed, my friend confided in me about how it felt to love a woman, then lose her. I selfishly pray that when the Lord calls Lena and me home, we go hand in hand. The idea of ever having to part with her sears my soul. And yes, I know God would comfort me, but I'd hate to consider such a separation. This morning as we laid him to rest beside his wife, I wondered if I had thanked him enough for his companionship. Aside from my beloved Lena, Dagget Shafer was my first real friend. God bless him.

twenty-one

Lena finished covering the rhubarb cobbler with a cloth. Caleb had taken a ham and a beef roast to the wagon, and Gabe carried a huge pot of greens. She corked the crockery jug filled with fresh buttermilk and glanced about to see if she'd missed anything. Spotting the quilt she'd set aside to spread out for their lunch, she snatched it up and wrapped it around the jug.

Taking a deep breath, she massaged the small of her back and blinked back the weariness threatening to creep into the eventful day—to say nothing of the queasiness attacking her stomach. *I have to tell Gabe soon. As observant as he is, I can't believe he doesn't already know.*

"Is there anything else?" Gabe asked from the doorway.

Instantly she drew her hands away from her back to gather up the food. "Just what I have here."

"You certainly look pretty this morning. Do weddings and house raisings always brighten your cheeks?" He warmed her heart with his irresistible smile.

I'm pregnant, Gabe, and tonight I'll tell you. "My how you toy with a woman's affections, Mr. Hunters. I'm overcome with your flattery."

He winked and snatched up the jug and cobbler. "I'll remember those sentiments."

She blushed and giggled. For a grown woman, sometimes the way Gabe made her feel like a schoolgirl nearly embarrassed her.

Today promised to be such fun. Amanda Shafer and the Reverend Jason Mercer had been married yesterday morning,

160

just one month after Dagget had died. The young minister declared his intentions shortly after the funeral, promising all he'd see to raising the Shafer children. Today, the community gathered together to build them a sod cabin.

Lena tingled with excitement. The mere thought of visiting with the women all day long pushed aside the sickness that had plagued her since earlier that morning. She'd stopped telling Gabe about the morning wave of illness until she knew for sure she carried their baby. The poor man didn't suspect a thing. She touched her stomach. The thought of new life, another child for Gabe, filled her with anticipation. But along with the joy came the reality of how lucky she'd been to give birth to two healthy boys who had aged beyond the critical years. She prayed her new baby would also thrive in this hard country.

Enough of these silly worries! Gabe will be so happy!

The wagon ride to the Shafers, now the Mercers and Shafers, seemed bumpier than usual, or perhaps the jolt rocked her queasy stomach. She continued to smile, praying her stomach to calm. Caleb and Simon hadn't done this to her. Perhaps she carried a girl. What a sweet, delicious thought.

With the musings rolling delightfully around in her head, she pushed away the sickness threatening to send her sprawling into the dirt. She could hear Gabe now—crowing like a lone rooster in a chicken house. And the boys, they'd be wonderful big brothers.

"Are you feeling all right?" Gabe asked, reaching over to take her hand into his.

Does he know? "I'm very happy," she replied.

"Happiness doesn't make one pale—or get sick."

Sometimes. "I'm perfectly fine," she assured him and reached over to plant a kiss on his cheek. "Today will be such fun. I can hardly wait."

"I agree. You can socialize with all the women while we

men build Amanda and the reverend's new home."

She laughed. "Are you wanting to trade places?"

"Absolutely not. Besides, you spent three years laboring in man's work, and I plan to do everything in my power to make sure your life never involves that again. Women's chores are difficult enough."

"You're too good to me. I'm not so sure I deserve you." She grinned up at the early morning sun. Birthing babies was hard work, but it was a whole sight easier than farming or building cabins. "I hope it's not too late when we get home today."

"It's hard to tell, Lena. Being new to this, I don't know how long it will take to construct the cabin, but I imagine a good many folks will show up to help."

She nodded, busily forming the words she'd use to tell Gabe about the baby. *Have you ever thought about a child of your own? No, he considers Caleb and Simon his own. Maybe, wouldn't it be grand to have a little one? Or, do you think you could build a cradle?* The thought of holding an infant again and watching him or her grow filled her with joy. God certainly had blessed her over and beyond what she'd ever imagined.

Gabe and Lena were among the first workers at the building site. Amanda and the reverend had chosen an area beyond the dugout to construct their home. Like so many other farmers, they planned to use the dugout for a barn as long as it stood. Gabe didn't think it would last beyond another winter.

Eager to get started, Gabe helped Lena unload the wagon.

"Go on, get going," she laughed. "Simon can help me. Never saw a man in my life who loved work more than you."

He leaned closer. "Oh, there're a few things I enjoy more."

She blushed and glanced about them. "Gabe Hunters, someone will hear you!"

Gabe grinned at his wife and watched her and Simon

unload food onto a makeshift table. He grabbed two spades for himself and Caleb and trekked toward the other men busy at work. The sod house would be approximately sixteen feet wide by twenty feet long, the size of most all the sod houses. Amanda claimed it would be a mansion in comparison to what she and her siblings were accustomed to.

"Mornin', Gabe, Caleb," a neighboring man greeted.

"Morning," he replied. Riley O'Connor walked with the man, but he didn't acknowledge Gabe or look his way.

I'm going to try to be civil. He can't help being lonely.

They hurried to a field of thick, strong sod where a few men turned over furrows for the sod bricks. Gabe watched in earnest, for he wanted to build a barn in the fall. He and Caleb helped trim the bricks to three feet long and two feet wide, understanding they must be equally cut to insure straight, solid walls.

"Sure glad you taught me how important it is to know arithmetic," Caleb said, measuring a sod brick with a piece of string Lena had cut for the occasion.

"Never underestimate the value of education," Gabe replied, tossing his elder son a grin. "Although experience is important too."

They shared a laugh, and as they worked side by side, Gabe reminded Caleb of the fall and winter and all the lessons the family had to teach him. So much there had been for Gabe to learn, and plenty more remained ahead.

The cabin raising went fairly quickly. The first row of bricks was laid along the foundation line, with younger children and some of the women filling the gaps with mud as mortar. Every third layer was laid crosswise to enforce the structure and bind it all together. They set in frames for a door and two windows and put aside sod to secure them later on. Shortly after noon, the walls stood nearly high enough for the roof, but tantalizing aromas from the food tables caused them all to stop and eat.

"Are you enjoying the day?" Gabe asked Lena, handing her his tin plate. He'd eaten in a rush so he could get back to work. As soon as all the men were finished, the women and children would share in the food.

Her eyes sparkled. "This is better than a church social. We've all brought Amanda gifts for her new home, and she's so very happy."

"What has she gotten?" Gabe asked curiously.

"Food, scented soap, embroidered pillowcases and handkerchiefs, a cornhusk basket, and some fabric scraps for a quilt. The poor girl has never known anyone to care for her like the reverend, and combined with the cabin and all, she's a little beside herself."

He stood and brushed the cornbread crumbs from his hands. "My compliments to all the women for their fine cooking." He winked and brushed her cheek with his thumb. How lovely she looked, his Lena. Her cheeks tinted pink and rosy, reminding him of wildflowers blossoming in the sun. The sky had seemed to dance with color, but not nearly as brilliant as the light in her eyes. "I love you," he whispered.

She wrinkled her nose. "I have something to tell you."

"And what is that?"

"Well, I—"

"Hey, Gabe, if you're done, how about giving me a hand with framing the roof?" a neighboring farmer called. "Since the preacher's gone to the trouble of having lumber hauled in, the least we can do is get it up right."

"I'll be right there." Gabe glanced at his wife, waiting for her to speak.

"I'll tell you later." Lena laughed. "The news can wait."

Gabe saw Caleb eating with a young man, laughing and talking, but at the sound of the neighbor's voice, Caleb glanced up.

"Finish your meal, Son. You've worked hard today." He

remembered his own longing for a companion when he was Caleb's age and how much he valued the friendships in Nebraska. Yes, he was a fairly lucky man, as they said in Nebrasky.

&

Leaning against the wagon, Lena crossed her arms and fought a wave of dizziness. She hadn't been able to eat all day for fear of being sick. Mercy, those boys hadn't made her ill like this, but soon she'd be four months along, and the sickness should leave.

"Are you all right?" Nettie Franklin asked. She'd helped Lena put her things back into the wagon.

"I'm fine," Lena assured her.

"You're pale, and I see you didn't eat a thing."

Lena nodded, nearly overflowing to tell someone about the baby. "Can you keep a secret for a day?"

The young woman quickly moved to her side. Her large, expressive eyes widened. "On a stack of Bibles, I'll keep a secret."

"I'm pregnant," Lena mouthed and looked around to make sure no one else had heard.

Nettie giggled. As the local midwife, she had a right to know about future babies. "So Gabe doesn't know?"

"Not yet. I started to tell him a few minutes ago, but Hank Culpepper hollered at him to come help with the roof." Lena wiggled her shoulders, the excitement of actually telling someone about the baby made her want to shout. "But I will tonight—if I don't bust first."

"Have you been sick much?"

Lena squeezed shut her eyes. "Every morning. What amazes me is Gabe usually doesn't miss a thing, and he has yet to question me. I can't believe he hasn't guessed it."

Nettie hugged her shoulders. "I'm so happy for you. What a blessing."

Suddenly, Lena felt her stomach roll. "What is that horrible smell?"

They looked to the cooking fire where a kettle of beans still simmered, but with the offensive odor Lena felt certain they'd burned.

The two scurried to pull the kettle from the fire. Another whiff of the beans sent Lena's stomach and head spinning. She swallowed the bile rising in her throat and blinked repeatedly to stop the dizziness. Blackness surrounded her. Nettie screamed for help just as Lena's world grew dark.

≥∂

Gabe wiped the sweat from his brow with the back of his shirt. Water would quench his powerful thirst. Besides, he was curious over Lena's news. He looked about and saw there was a lull in the work right now too. Maybe he could take this opportunity to satisfy both desires.

"Be right back," Gabe called out, thinking how his vocabulary had shrunk since last October. But he fit in with these farmers because now he belonged.

Lifting his hat to cool his head, Gabe headed toward the spot he'd left Lena. Some kind of commotion had drawn the ladies' attention. Rounding a group of wagons, he moved closer.

Suddenly, Gabe felt the color drain from his face. All of his worst nightmares and misgivings about his wife were vividly realized in front of his eyes. Rage seethed from the pores of his flesh.

Lena lay in the arms of Riley O'Connor.

twenty-two

"What is going on here?" Gabe bellowed. He clenched his fist, ready to send it through those pearly white teeth.

The crowd of women around Lena and Riley instantly hushed and made way for Gabe to reach his wife. He'd tear Riley apart with his bare hands. So this was Lena's news! All those words of love and endearing smiles meant nothing to her. *Lord, help me!*

"Riley, what are you doing with my wife?" he shouted.

Riley looked up. Surprise swept across his face. Gabe took a glimpse of Lena, who moved slightly in Riley's arms. She looked pale, ghastly pale, but no wonder. She'd been discovered.

"Answer me, Man." Gabe pushed his way through the mounting crowd. The women gasped. If they wanted to see a fight, then he'd give them one.

Listen, Gabe. It's not what you think.

He held his breath and attempted to control his rapid breathing.

Nettie rushed to his side. "No, Gabe. This is not what it seems. Lena fainted, and if it hadn't been for Riley, she'd have fallen into the fire."

His head pounded. Had he heard correctly?

"That's right, Hunters," Riley said. "I caught her before she fell. Nothing else."

"Gabe," Lena moaned. "Where's Gabe?"

Emotion clawed at his throat and threatened to choke him alive. Riley lifted Lena into Gabe's arms without a word. She felt light, fragile. "Lena, are you all right?" He didn't care that most of Archerville gawked at him. He'd already made a fool of himself— not once thinking about Lena, but only of himself. "I'm so sorry I shouted."

"I didn't hear a thing," she said and wet her lips. "I don't remember what happened to me, just got dizzy."

"Well, I'm getting you home and to bed. Tomorrow I'm riding to North Bend for the doctor. No more of this."

"No. It's not necessary. I'm fine, really." She stirred slightly, but he could see through her ploy. "This is natural, Gabe. The sickness will pass."

"What do you mean the sickness will. . ." He heard Nettie laugh, then slowly the other women began to laugh. "Are we? I mean, are you?"

Lena smiled and reached up to touch his face. "Yes, Gabe. We're going to have a baby."

"Ah, wh. . .when?"

"Mid-December."

He let out a shout that resembled a war whoop he'd heard at a Wild West show back East.

"Gabe Hunters," she laughed. "You sound just like a Nebrasky farmer."

❧

On December 10, Gabe paced the cabin floor while Caleb and Simon stared into the fire. Lena had labored with the baby for nearly four hours, and he'd had enough. She didn't cry out, but he'd heard her whimperings. Outside, the night was exceptionally cold, although only a sprinkling of snow lay on the ground.

"How much longer?" Caleb asked, breaking the silence from the ticking clock above the fireplace.

"Soon," Gabe muttered. "Can't be much longer."

He went back to pacing, keeping time with the clock. In the next moment, he heard a cry. He stopped cold and stared at the quilt leading into their bedroom.

"You have a girl, Gabe Hunters!" Nettie Franklin called. "A healthy baby girl!"

"Can I come in now?" he asked, frozen in his spot. "I want to see my wife and baby."

"Not just yet. Give me a moment," Nettie replied. "Oh, she's right pretty, but no hair."

Gabe waited for what he believed was an hour. Suddenly he couldn't contain his excitement a moment longer. He pushed through the quilt, his gaze drinking in the sight of his lovely Lena and the red-faced baby in her arms.

"She's beautiful," he whispered, tears springing to his eyes. "And you're beautiful." He kissed Lena's damp forehead, then her lips, before kneeling beside the bed.

Lena glanced up from staring into the baby's face. "Thank You, Lord," she whispered.

"Amen," he said, gingerly picking up a perfect, tiny hand. The awe of this miracle left him speechless. He memorized every bit of the tiny face, then kissed the baby's cheek. "I love you, Lena. You never cease to fill my days with joy."

"And I love you. She looks like you."

"Oh, I want her to look like you."

"Nonsense. She has your eyes and chin. They're just like her father's. I certainly hope she doesn't have my temper."

Gabe chuckled. "I want my daughter to have spunk."

"I'll settle for spunk. What shall we name her?" Lena asked.

He pressed his lips together. "Hmm. How do you feel about naming her after our mothers?"

Her eyes widened. "I think that's a wonderful idea."

"I've been thinking the best way for me to honor my mother is to name my daughter after her. What was your mother's name?"

"Cynthia."

"Cynthia Marie. What do you think?"

"Perfect," Lena said with a smile.

"Caleb, Simon. Come on in and meet Miss Cynthia Marie Hunters, your new sister."

Gabe's eyes pooled with joy. The Lord had showered him with so many blessings. Surely something he'd never have known from books. The intensity of his feelings for Lena and his family spread through him like sweet molasses. Never had he expected the love of such a fine woman, or two strapping sons, or the sweetness of an infant daughter. He was happy. He was content. He'd given and received the greatest gift of all.

A Letter To Our Readers

Dear Reader:

In order that we might better contribute to your reading enjoyment, we would appreciate your taking a few minutes to respond to the following questions. We welcome your comments and read each form and letter we receive. When completed, please return to the following:

Rebecca Germany, Fiction Editor
Heartsong Presents
PO Box 719
Uhrichsville, Ohio 44683

1. Did you enjoy reading *Mail-Order Bride* by DiAnn Mills?
   ❏ Very much! I would like to see more books by this author!
   ❏ Moderately. I would have enjoyed it more if

   _____

   _____

   _____

2. Are you a member of **Heartsong Presents**?   ❏ Yes   ❏ No
   If no, where did you purchase this book? _____

   _____

3. How would you rate, on a scale from 1 (poor) to 5 (superior), the cover design? _____

4. On a scale from 1 (poor) to 10 (superior), please rate the following elements.

   ____ Heroine   ____ Plot
   ____ Hero   ____ Inspirational theme
   ____ Setting   ____ Secondary characters

6. How has this book inspired your life?_____

_____

_____

7. What settings would you like to see covered in future
   Heartsong Presents books? _____

_____

_____

8. What are some inspirational themes you would like to see
   treated in future books? _____

_____

_____

9. Would you be interested in reading other **Heartsong
   Presents** titles?   ❑ Yes   ❑ No

10. Please check your age range:
    ❑ Under 18   ❑ 18-24
    ❑ 25-34   ❑ 35-45
    ❑ 46-55   ❑ Over 55

Name_____

Occupation _____

Address _____

City_____ State_____ Zip_____

E-mail _____

A CURRIER
&IVES
CHRISTMAS

*T*he artistry of renowned lithographers Currier & Ives captures the beauty and nostalgia of simpler days and Christmases past.

Inspired by the classic American art of Currier & Ives, these seasonal love stories delve deep inside the artists' portrayals to imagine and illustrate the untold tales behind each wintry scene.

Look beyond the art to discover the heartwarming stories of holiday love of yesteryear in *A Currier & Ives Christmas*.

Historical, paperback, 352 pages, 5 ³⁄₁₆" x 8"

♥ • ♥ • ♥ • ♥ • ♥ • ❤ • ♥ • ♥ • ♥ • ♥ • ♥

♥ • ♥ • ♥ • ♥ • ♥ • ❤ • ♥ • ♥ • ♥ • ♥ • ♥

·······Presents·······

Hearts♥ng Presents
Love Stories Are Rated G!

That's for godly, gratifying, and of course, great! If you love a thrilling love story but don't appreciate the sordidness of some popular paperback romances, **Heartsong Presents** is for you. In fact, **Heartsong Presents** is the *only inspirational romance book club* featuring love stories where Christian faith is the primary ingredient in a marriage relationship.

Sign up today to receive your first set of four never-before-published Christian romances. Send no money now; you will receive a bill with the first shipment. You may cancel at any time without obligation, and if you aren't completely satisfied with any selection, you may return the books for an immediate refund!

Imagine. . .four new romances every four weeks—two historical, two contemporary—with men and women like you who long to meet the one God has chosen as the love of their lives. . .all for the low price of $10.99 postpaid.

To join, simply complete the coupon below and mail to the address provided. **Heartsong Presents** romances are rated G for another reason: They'll arrive *Godspeed!*

YES! Sign me up for Heartsong!

NEW MEMBERSHIPS WILL BE SHIPPED IMMEDIATELY!
Send no money now. We'll bill you only $10.99 post-paid with your first shipment of four books. Or for faster action, call1-800-847-8270 or visit www.heartsongpresents.com.

NAME _____

ADDRESS _____

CITY _____ STATE _____ ZIP _____

MAIL TO: Heartsong Presents, PO Box721, Uhrichsville, Ohio 44683

YES5-02